May the ~
bless you.

Cookies, Cocoa, and Capers

Laurie Boulden

Laurie Boulden

1

"St. Ives, I watch you in the pale moon gleaming. Beneath flakes of snow now streaming." Millicent, Millie to all who knew her, sang softly in the early morning darkness as poofs of snow drifted around her from the deep silvery night sky. After locking the house, she pressed the button in her pocket, and her SUV started. It was still cold when she slid into the driver's seat. She closed the door and then rubbed her hands together. The car was a few minutes from warming up. "Should have remembered gloves, girl." The dark quiet of the hour between four and five in the morning infused her with energy, more so than a cup of coffee. She watched the darkness around her. Patches of grass were now iced in white. "Not even Thanksgiving and we've already had snow." She chatted with herself. The blue light on the dashboard finally went out, and she got on her way.

A few minutes later, she turned onto Mainstreet. Three years ago, city council replaced the utilitarian streetlights with glossy black lampposts reminiscent of an old English village. The snow had ceased. Light from the posts glowed yellow from one end of the commercial district to the other. Everything was closed, of course. She glanced at the time on the radio. Four-twenty-eight. Plenty of time to prep the morning run of bakery goods.

She turned at the first cross street, then turned again into the rear parking lot. Serviceable lights lit the area. Millie pulled into the row adjacent to the bakery. A minute later, the night police cruiser entered the lot. Millie waved as she grabbed her purse and bag of groceries.

He rolled down his window. "Looks like all we'll get is a light dusting."

"Morning, Uncle Doe." Millie smiled as she searched her purse for the key to the back door of the bakery. He wasn't a true uncle, but she'd known him most of her life. "I'll have a fresh pan of cinnamon buns coming out of the oven at seven."

"With a nice hot cup of coffee?"

"Won't that keep you up?"

He laughed. "Nothing can stop this old man from snoring."

"Then hot coffee it is. See you soon." Millie turned the lock, opened the wide metal door, and reached around the edge for the lights. A moment later, the alarm was off, and Millie placed a large flour bin outside the door before locking herself inside the bakery.

Millie shrugged out of her coat and hung it on the first hook of the hall tree. She pulled open the locker at the base of the tree and dropped her purse inside. Once closed, she twisted the combination lock. The hall led to the main kitchen. Unlike the traditional bakery kitchens she'd used at school and the different venues for apprenticeships, this kitchen had the flare of design and class. Millie walked to the first stretch of cabinets with gray-veined white marble counters and dropped the bag of groceries. "Cinnamon, cinnamon," she muttered, digging through the blue canvas bag. "Ah-ha," she cheered as she wrapped her hand around the jar of the fresh-ground Indian spice.

After a walk through one of the fridges and a back-storage room, Millie placed the ingredients for buns on the counter. She pushed up on her toes to select one of the aprons folded on the open shelf above her station. Her white choice had a single turkey at the bottom trying to run away.

"Oh turkey day, oh turkey day, how much I love your dressing," she sang to the tune of a Christmas carol. After a few more made-up verses, large bowls held the main ingredients for the cinnamon buns. She opened the Indian spice, breathed the waft of scent rising into the air, then took a pinch and sprinkled it across the flour. "Ah, today's delectable ingredient." She walked across the kitchen and pulled a mixing stand back to her first station. While those ingredients were mixing, she unwrapped sticks of butter.

The other two stations were prepared quickly. Millie kept an eye on the ovens as she rolled mincemeat across the stainless-steel counter on the far end of the kitchen. The cold outside was forgotten as warmth from the ovens and the fresh smell of bread baking filled the air. Millie's sister, Stella, joined her. "Heavenly donuts, the smell of all this yumminess is making my mouth water."

Millie laughed. "Sure, get here after all the hard work is done."

Stella tossed her head and grinned. "Impeccable

timing as usual. I'll work on inventory, how's that?"

"Just until the gingerbread men are cooled enough to get iced. You'll have to make the icing."

"Shake of a leg." She glanced at her watch. "I'll have them ready by eight."

"Don't forget."

"Who, me?"

Both sisters laughed.

A few minutes before seven, Millie slid a hot roll onto a small dish, using a spoon to scrape a few dribbles of gooey sauce to pour over it. She pushed through the swinging door into the front room of the bakery. Although the open sign remained off, Uncle Doe's place was set, and she'd just poured a cup of coffee when he entered. He hung his heavy coat on a hook near the door. "Snow's stopped. Should have a peaceful morning commute."

"Commute?" Millie chuckled. "Stop signs along Mainstreet don't back anyone up, do they?"

"It's all relative. A few cars here is the same as a jam in Minneapolis."

She shook her head. "I'll gladly take St. Ives any day." She turned as the door opened again. "Mrs. Wethers. What can I get for you today?"

The older woman rubbed her arms. "It's Wednesday. My little chicks will be expecting cookies."

"I have Mexican wedding and lemon-doodles."

"Lemons will be lovely."

Millie reached under the counter for a bag. "I'll get these together then add it to your tab. What letter are they working on this week?"

"Well, I'm saving "t" for Thanksgiving so we're

making words that have 'v'."

"V is for victory," Millie folded the bag and handed it to Mrs. Wethers. "I'll be baking turkey cookies next week, so I'll be sure to save you some."

Early baking completed as the sun rose. Millie arranged display trays with the goods that were ready. She set most in the tall stacks behind the register but saved the best for the window display. She placed the pan of gingerbread snaps in the window, breathing in the enticing aroma of cinnamon and molasses. Satisfied the pan sat parallel with the snickerdoodles, she straightened and caught the eye of Baxter Dane through the glass. She tried not to let her smile falter, but Dane didn't even offer a slight upturn of lip. Millie held his stare until he turned away, most likely heading for his store, Book Shop.

"Like that's an intriguing name," Millie muttered as she left the display case, willing the flutter in her chest to calm. He rankled her feathers, as Grandma Cooke liked to say.

Millie flipped the switch for the sign as she passed near the front door. The familiar buzz of neon barely registered. Bake-n-Cake Bakery and Café glowed. The sign had a cupcake with pink icing on top, but Bake-n-Cake was known for lots of goodies, not just cake.

Millie started to whistle as she headed toward the kitchen. The opening door and brush of cold air caused her to turn back.

"I'm sorry," Allison Granger gushed as she hurried into the bakery while pulling off her jacket. Her purse slipped from her arm, and the flower-encrusted bag spilled across the black and white checkered floor. "Oh, no." She sank beside her purse, shoving things back inside. "I'm so sorry, Miss Millie. Won't happen again."

Millie grinned. "Wouldn't matter." She picked up a tube of lipstick and handed it to Allison. "If I did away with you, Aunt Lettie wouldn't let me hear the end of it."

"It does help I'm her only granddaughter." Allison's smile eased to a more-natural fit as she stood, belongings returned to their rightful place. She moved the doorbell over the door into place before crossing the café.

"And she's best friends with our grandmother." Millie repeated the familiar phrase. The door jangled with their first patron. "You're also good with customers." She held the hinged counter section to let Allison step through. "Let's have a sweet morning. The specialty brew is Santa's Secret."

Millie entered the kitchen. She drew her fingers along the white countertop as she crossed to a buzzing oven. With one hand on the handle, she peeked through the window. Golden brown men filled the tray. She pushed the timer and opened the oven, grabbing a mitt to pull the gingerbread men from their cave. She slid the pan onto a shelf in the cooling rack. Four other pans were already cool enough to touch. But, looking at the empty crock on the counter, she frowned.

"Stella? I thought you were going to have icing ready by now." Millie hollered.

A bump in the back closet alerted Millie to her sister's location. She brushed her hands on her apron, frowning with the turkey, and headed toward the noise. Stella had herself on the second rung of a ladder, facing away from the ladder and leaning against the rungs behind her. She held a clipboard in one hand and a pencil in the other, reaching up to count the number of bags of sugar. She slid her black retro glasses up as she recorded a number.

"Uh, Stell?" Millie leaned against the open door of the supply closet.

"Almost done." She looked back up.

"Icing? Ring a bell? We want to get the men in the window. Can't do that without dressing them first."

"Icing?" Stella glanced at the slim leather watch on her left wrist. "But its… oh, after eight already."

Allison's call from the other end of the kitchen pulled Millie from her sister. "Hey, you gals got time to take a cake order? I'm swamped up here."

Millie turned back to Stella. "I'll take the cake order. Get the icing done." Millie turned to leave then swung back around. "Icing now, you can complete the inventory later today."

Stella stepped down the ladder and offered a sassy grin. "I'll give them speedos."

Millie walked away shaking her head. Though they were sisters, Stella was petite with dark curly hair, almond-shaped glasses, and a glimmering smile. Brilliant and forgetful was how most people described her.

What about me? Millie caught a glimpse of her round face as she pushed through the door into the café space. Her brown hair had a wave. She shared the same hazel eyes as Stella. Otherwise, Millie was a little taller, a little rounder, and more inclined to pay attention to all the details. Like icing.

She grinned at the woman next to the open cake book. A toddler straddled her side and a young girl reached up in front to try to see.

"You want to see the cakes?"

The little girl's head bounced emphatically. Millie laughed, nabbing the stool beneath the counter. "This belongs to my sister, but since she's not here right now..." Millie winked as mom took the stool with a grateful smile. "Someone having a birthday?" Millie asked as the little girl climbed the step and leaned on the counter, elbows bent to rest her chin in her cupped hands.

Mom grinned, tugging at one of the golden curls on the girl's head. "This one is turning four. Finally, old enough to want a special cake."

The girl gasped as she turned a page. "This one! Can we do this one?" More pages turned. "Oh, no. This one. This is the one. Can we do this one?"

After the fifth exclamation, the little girl looked at her mother with her mouth hanging open and eyes wide. The two adults laughed. Millie patted her hand. "How many people are going to want cake?"

The little girl looked around. "Doesn't everyone?"

"Not here, silly. Are you having a party or family?"

"We'll save the party until kindergarten." Mom held up a hand. "Just family. Grandma and Gramps are coming, that makes six of us."

Millie flipped the book back to the princess cake. "This is perfect for six. What do you think?"

The girl tilted her head and then nodded.

"What's your favorite color?"

"Pepper."

Millie opened her mouth. Of course, pepper would be a color to a four-year-old. "I don't have icing that color." She turned the flap on the page open. "What do you think of pink? Or this blue?"

The girl put her finger on the pink princess. "Can you make her sparkle?"

"I can." Millie assured, then turned her attention to mom. "When do you want the cake?"

The woman adjusted the child on her hip, leaned toward Millie, and lowered her voice. "Is there any possible way to get it today? I meant to drop in last week, but one thing drives out another…" She blinked.

Millie placed her hand on the woman's arm. "I have supplies prepped just in case. The princess cake will be ready by two this afternoon." Millie grinned at the little girl. "Should I write Susie on the cake?"

The girl tilted her head. "Who's that?"

"Why, you, isn't it?"

She giggled. "I not Susie."

Millie tapped her finger on her nose. "Hm, Becky. Or maybe Mary?"

"I Jessie." She slapped her hands on the counter.

"Why, that's the perfect name. Jessie. I like it."

"Thank you so much. I better get this little one to preschool. I wanted to make sure we stopped, and I didn't forget again."

"I'll see you this afternoon."

Millie grinned as she closed the lid on the glittering princess cake.

"That is adorable," Stella said as she hopped onto the counter beside her. "Did you take pictures for our Facebook page?"

Millie rolled her eyes. "Facebook requires time and effort. Where's that supposed to come from?"

"It would be good for business."

"Business is good now. When we're able to hire more staff, we'll dive into social media." Millie swatted Stella's knee. "Until then…" She shrugged.

"You're too young to be a dinosaur." Stella jumped from the counter. She blew a bubble of gum and popped it against her teeth.

Millie twirled a pink hand towel, debating if her sister was close enough for her to snap.

"I see you." Stella skipped away.

"Did you get the Christmas calendar up? We've got orders coming in already. Thanksgiving is next week."

Allison distracted them. "Can either of you hop down to Christine's? They placed an order but I'm heading to class."

"I think we're going to need seasonal help." Millie toyed with the towel in her hand.

"I can ask in class. I'm certain there must be at least one college student who needs money for the holidays. Until then, can one of you take the order to the beauty shop?"

"I'll go." Millie turned to Stella. "Watch the front?"

She nodded. "Let me grab…"

"Later." Both Millie and Allison said. Millie stood against the swinging door. "You can straighten the tables if no one comes in."

Blue sky didn't keep the mid November temps from dropping. Millie tried to roll her shoulders to get the top of her coat closed, but her full hands didn't help her succeed. She stepped around a sign on the sidewalk and angled her way to Christine's beauty shop. One of the girls was watching, and she thankfully walked through an open door into warmth.

"You are a blessing," Christine hurried from her

client to grab the drink carton and hug Millie. She gave a laugh. "Has the temperature dropped? Your cheek is frozen."

"Colder than when I came in this morning." Millie smiled as she handed over the bag of cookies. "Figured you were busy. Be sure to tell everyone where to get their Christmas cookies."

The large woman in the middle chair waved. "Like we don't know Bake-n-Cake?"

"Glad to hear it." Millie waved. "See you all later."

The air had cooled. Millie pulled the collar of her jacket around her neck. She glanced at the sign on the sidewalk as she passed. A few steps later, the words on the sign registered. "Cookies and cocoa for Christmas?" Millie froze, turned around, and scowled. The top of the sign had the Book Shop logo set among a shelf of books. On the lines beneath were the words she thought she'd seen. *Since when does Book Shop have cookies?* She looked in the window. The round table was draped in a fabric cloth with muted holly and poinsettias. In the middle, rose a large tree formed by books stacked on each other in a variety of angles. Two places were set on either side of the tree: teacups with large marshmallows sticking over the rim and a green plate with snickerdoodle cookies. The window looked enticing. *How could he?* She glared into the dark beyond but didn't see Dane.

Millie stomped back to the café. Rubbing hands together, she crossed the room to where Stella organized straws, sugar, and napkins on a side bar. "That brat of a bookstore owner has the nerve to try to sell cookies. Next door to a bakery, and he hasn't asked us to provide them."

Stella turned. "What do you mean, sell cookies? Did he hire girl scouts?"

"He's got a display with plates of cookies and hot chocolate." She looked at their window. *At least our cookies have character.* Stella had decorated the gingerbread men in a variety of European outfits.

"It's a ploy to get people into the bookstore. Everyone in town knows we have the best cookies. And cakes." Stella rubbed the cotton cloth in her hand across the back of the cupcake sign. "I just sent princess on her way."

"Still, it's not the thing to do. How would he like it if we set up a corner bookshelf and sold bestsellers?"

Stella scrunched her face as she studied the corner. Millie rolled her eyes and swatted her sister's arm. "We aren't going into the book business. The bakery is plenty of business to keep track of."

"Oh. Maybe you can try something else to get his attention."

Millie looked out at the bright, cold afternoon. *Perhaps we should. He obviously meant to get my attention.* "But what." She tapped her chin.

"Which what?"

"What do we do?"

Stella looked out the window, and then her mouth widened into a slow smile. She slid her glance to Millie, and Millie couldn't keep herself from smiling as well. Stella had an idea. "What?"

"Let me see the sign."

They walked outside. Millie gasped at the cold and wrapped her arms around herself.

"It's bloody cold out here," Stella turned to go back inside.

Millie pulled her toward the sign. "It's right there. What's your idea?"

"We get chalk." Her teeth chattered.

Millie rolled her eyes and let Stella lead them back indoors. "Graffiti?"

Stella shook her head. "Spelling. What if we change a couple of the words?"

It would be risky. They'd have to do it when he wasn't likely to be watching. "Saturday morning, he does the children's reading hour." Millie smirked. "Might be afternoon before he realizes there's a problem with his sign."

2

"Good morning, Miss Millie." Allison skipped into the bakery Saturday morning, followed by a young woman. "Angela came with me. Do you have time for a quick sit down?"

Millie slipped through the partition. "Take the counter and I'll be happy to." She crossed the room and held her hand to Angela. "How are you?"

"Great. I love this place."

Millie laughed. "I won't argue with you. How do you know Allison?"

"We're in class together. I might have pushed a few chairs over when she said you're hiring for the season."

"What about when school's out? That's usually the beginning of December. I'll need someone who can stay through the New Year."

"Oh, that's me, for sure. Mom decided to go to Florida to visit her sisters. I told her I'd rather stay here, and the apartment complex said I can keep my place until the end of May."

"Have you worked in a café or restaurant before?"

"Yes, like every summer since I turned sixteen. My uncle had a pizza shop."

"Here's what I can pay." Millie handed Angela a

card. "Hours are mostly weekends. You and Allison can decide if you want to switch some of the morning shifts, if you're available."

Angela nodded. "Nice thing about being a junior is I don't have to take those eight a.m. classes. Thank you, I can't wait to learn something about baking."

"We bake everything on site, so you should be able to pick up a thing or two. Did you want to get started now? You can shadow Allison. She'll help you figure out how to use the register."

The two girls bounced with excitement when Angela shared the news. Millie grinned at Allison. Good choice.

A glance at her watch showed a few minutes to nine. "I'm taking a coffee run over to the salon," she hollered as she set four paper cups in a drink holder. She buttoned up her coat before heading outside. She kept her head downward to keep some of the cold wind off her face, but she still managed a glance at the bookstore. Two mothers stood by the table in the window. By the time she returned a few minutes later, they had wandered off. Feigning dropping something on the sidewalk, Millie crouched beside the sign. Surreptitious glances showed the coast was clear. She smudged a letter and then used the piece of chalk in her pocket to turn an e to an a. She managed a few more letter changes before wiping her fingers on her brown thigh-length jacket and heading back to the bakery. She whistled as she pushed through the door, trying to match the chime of its bell. Stella, wiping the back corner of counter, turned and lifted her brows. Millie simply smiled, heading for the kitchen. Time to bake more cookies.

Morning busied. Allison leaned into the kitchen with a cheery greeting as Millie pulled a pan of snickerdoodles from the oven. "Oh, good. The window's looking bare. Everyone's gearing up for the holiday next week."

"For that we are thankful." Stella interjected as she crossed the kitchen.

Allison and Millie groaned. Millie tested one of the cooling cookies then pointed at Allison. "Consolidate what's left in the window and bring me the empty trays. Make it look nice, of course. How's Angela doing?"

"She knows her stuff. I think you'll like her."

"Get those trays for me," Millie directed as another beep sounded on the ovens.

It didn't take long for Millie to have fresh trays prepped. She backed through the swinging kitchen door, hands full once more. The window display had two shelves. She knelt and placed the new trays on the bottom, giving a twist until she was satisfied the best view would be from the street. A man wearing brown slacks and black boots stopped. *Caught a customer quick,* Millie thought as she looked up, but then her stomach flopped. Dane stood in front of the window. From the look in his eye, he knew about the sign and had a pretty good idea who was responsible. Millie tried to control the twitch in her lips. *Horrible liar.* The urge to giggle made her bite on her upper lip. She swiftly closed the display, stood, and turned away. But not before seeing Dane shake his head.

She crossed to the counter, taking a deep breath.

Stella finished pouring a cup of coffee before turning to Millie. "Was that?"

Millie nodded, not bothering to hide her wide smile.

"Who, dear?" Aunt Lettie lifted a cup and saucer, causing a rattle.

Millie took it from her. "Your usual seat?"

The elderly woman nodded. "Bea and Sylvia should be along in a minute. They wanted to find out what Mr. Dane means by Christmas Keys. Must be a tale he's discovered in one of those old books of his, but I don't know."

Ah, the widow peeps were responsible for revealing changes to the sign. They were a harmless group, known for peeping their noses into everyone's business. And everyone made sure they were safe. Millie didn't mind Dane knowing. The gleam in his eye still caused a flutter in her stomach.

"Are you alright, dear?" Aunt Lettie patted her hand.

"Fine. What kind of pie will you want with Thanksgiving?"

Her face brightened. "Hugh will be here. I thought he'd have a wife with him, but something happened, and he isn't getting married. Will you have your cinnamon apple spice? I think that was his favorite."

"I'd be run out of town if I didn't bake cinnamon spice pies. Ah, here comes more of your group." Millie waved them over. "I'll get your coffees. Is today an extra cream day, Aunt Dahlia?"

The tallest of the Widow Peeps nodded. "This much cold this early in the season? We'll need an extra layer of fat to survive winter." Dahlia's southern drawl made the words laya and winta.

"I prefer my fat in the shape of a gingerbread man," Aunt Bea sat beside Aunt Lettie.

Millie went to fix the order for the Aunts. Angela

pulled a serving tray from under the counter. She put a lace liner on the tray. "Are they all sisters?"

"No. Aunt Bea and Grandma Cooke, um, Sylvia, are sisters. They're on mom's side. Allison is Aunt Lettie's granddaughter."

"But you call her aunt as well?"

"Everyone calls them Aunts." She glanced at the table in the far corner where the Widow Peeps chose to settle. "They're harmless. You might hear people refer to them as the Widow Peeps."

"That's sad."

"They've turned it into a positive." Millie steamed milk before pouring it into Aunt Dahlia's coffee. "They're well known along Mainstreet. If you ever need something or want to find something out, ask any of them."

Stella stepped close, nudging her. "They ratted us out, didn't they?" She glanced over Millie's shoulder toward the group.

"Not on purpose." Millie added a plate with four gingerbread men dressed in German lederhosen.

"Well, no more time for capers until after the holidays. We get a rest tomorrow and have nearly two hundred pies to bake by Wednesday."

3

Millie shivered as cold seeped through her jacket. "It's only mid-November," she muttered, digging in a pocket for the key to the back door of the bakery. The security light overhead provided a comfortable circle in the predawn darkness. Once the door opened, she reached around and turned on the kitchen lights.

Quiet surrounded her. There was the usual hum of the freezers, but other than that, the new day waited silently for her to start it. Millie locked the door behind her as she unwrapped her navy scarf from around her neck. She looped the scarf on one of the hooks hanging above four wooden lockers. She dropped her purse in its usual place and twisted the dial.

A song she'd heard on the drive came to mind as she pulled an industrial mixer onto the counter. She sang a few lines while she prepped for Thanksgiving pies needing to be baked.

Not much later, a few dozen shells cooling on the rack and the first vat of pumpkin spice pie filling whirling down, Millie heard her name being called from the front.

"Mills," Stella's voice tinged with frustration.

Millie wiped her hands on her apron and scooted to the swinging door, using her hip to push through. "What on earth is the problem?" The first thing she noticed entering the dining room was the deep orange glow.

Stella still held her white woolen muffler with one hand. "Did you see the front when you came in?"

"What do you mean?" Millie checked the tables draped in round Christmas-themed cloths. Nothing seemed amiss among the sporadic arrangement of tables through the room. Then she saw the winter window display with an oddly orange sky. "What did you do to the window?"

Stella placed her muffler and matching scarf on a nearby table. "*I* didn't do anything."

Millie pointed. "The sky is orange."

"Oh," Stella shook her head. "It isn't just the sky."

Millie frowned. Evergreen trees on a snow-covered hill had been painted across the inside of the main window over the weekend. The smaller window on the other side of the door continued the hill and most of a red sleigh with silver bells filled the rest of the window. Millie's jaw dropped. Was that the head of a skeleton rising from the sleigh? "What happened?"

"You have to see it from outside to get the full effect."

Millie didn't bother with a coat. She burst through the front door. The jangle overhead marked the embrace of cold. Though daylight had not yet reached its full potential, the window scene was unmistakable.

From the outside, the forest hill was a black slope with rudimentary tombstones. The sky was indeed orange with a pumpkin sun. A skeleton had been drawn leaning against the sleigh. Had it been Halloween rather than days before Thanksgiving… her mind stopped working.

Stella bumped against her, throwing a coat across Millie's shoulders. "It's actually quite creative if you think about it."

"What? How could someone… why would …"

"The detail." Stella gasped, impressed. "Mind if I take a picture?"

Millie's glance must have spoken because Stella drooped her head. Millie rubbed her eyes, but the image remained. "Who would paint over our window like this?"

Stella giggled, which only made Millie's angst deepen. "What is funny? Winter wonderland is ruined. What am I supposed to do with this?" She waved her hand, tears prickling her eyes.

Stella pushed her glasses up. "Nothing's ruined. This is on the outside and the other is inside."

"I should call the police."

Stella laughed. "And tell them what? An artist painted your front windows?"

"We can't let people see this, but there's no time to fix it." She tried to breath as she wrung her hands. "Call Allison. The two of you can tape butcher paper over it. We'll say it's a surprise, a special surprise for after Thanksgiving."

"It's a surprise alright. He's quite brilliant, really."

"He who? Who's brilliant?"

"Who do you think?" Stella looked down the street.

Millie frowned and glanced as well. No one else seemed to be in yet. That was good. There might be… Dane? He did this? Why would he? "That wretched feeble-minded book bum."

Stella held up a hand. "Not that I'm on his side, but you did start the prank."

"Me? He's selling baking goods like he's a Barnes and Noble. Get Allison. I've got pies that need to go in the oven."

Millie seethed as she dumped pumpkin mixture into the pie shells.

"Those pies are going to be full of grumble," Stella sang as she hurried through the kitchen. "Allison's here. Just grabbing the butcher paper roll and scissors."

She was gone a moment later, but Millie stopped. Rows of pies filled the counter, six to a cookie sheet. The orange mixture reminded her of the painted window, but Stella was right. "Bake with a bad attitude and everyone feels bad." She quoted the line her grandmother learned from her great aunt. "Fine. I'm not going to have a bad attitude." She sprinkled a touch of cinnamon sugar on each of the pies and added her customary dollop of heavy whipped cream in the center. "Now you can be as sweet as me," she mumbled as she placed the first sheet in the oven.

Less than half an hour, the smell of pumpkin pie wafted through the bakery. Millie moved a rolling cart from the kitchen to the front in order to set the trays of donuts, cookies, and apple treats where they belonged. Stella and Allison had most of the front windows covered. The dining area seemed dim, although not the orangey hint it had been earlier. Orange sky and the skeleton were still visible. As were the shapes shadowing the trees on the hill. Obviously, the window had been painted after the hired designer had finished inside for the day. Had Dane spent the night, the very-unusual-for-November cold night, painting? Stupid man, "I hope he gets pneumonia."

"What?"

Stella was closer than she realized. "Nothing. Thinking aloud, which is never a good idea. You'll have to cover the inside as well. Hopefully the weather will warm up by Thursday and we can figure out how to get this off."

"Thursday's Thanksgiving."

"And it's the only time we can be assured no one will be shopping on Mainstreet. I'm going to check the pies."

Stella drummed up a few lamps, and by the time Millie took a break from pies, the dining area had a nice murmur of conversations from their customers and plenty of light.

"It's the dullest Christmas wrapping I've ever seen," a large elderly woman with lavender hair set in three distinct waves hugged Millie.

"Grandma Cooke! What are you doing here?"

"I know." She widened her gray eyes. "One would think an early chill like this would make these old bones ache like the dickens, but I declare I am right as rain. Or snow."

Millie hugged her back. "Most of us are happy to wait for snow until closer to Christmas. Want your usual?"

Grandma Cooke patted her cheek. "Of course. I'll sit by the fireplace. A nice touch for a day like today."

"Is your Mr. Willard joining you?"

She sighed dramatically. "Alas, my Mr. Willard is on his way to Grand Forks to have Thanksgiving with his family. I told him waiting until Tuesday was a mistake, what with traffic and everything, but he insisted. Or rather, his son insisted, and he thought it best to go."

"Don't you worry, he'll only be in the car a few hours." Millie turned to fix a cup of hot tea for Grandma Cooke and decided on a mug of Santa's Special for herself. She placed the cups on the table and sat across from the woman who had encouraged the sisters to complete school after their parents died.

"Your sister says you'll be working part of Thursday."

"We'll still be home to help with dinner. You'll be with us at Aunt Bea's, right??"

"I hope she has room for all of us?"

Millie lifted her brows. "What do you mean? Her dining table sits twelve."

"Bea invited a few of her neighbors. And Dahlia's nephew doesn't have anywhere to go. Leticia and her grandchildren. I insisted." She shook her head. "They wanted to take her to a restaurant, like they'd have anything half as good as us."

"Maybe the guys want to watch football."

"We'll turn on the tv in the den. The men can hang out there if they like."

Grandma Cooke continued speaking, but Millie's attention turned to the man walking through the door. His short hair was more silver than blonde. He wore his brown jacket buttoned, collar raised, hands shoved in pockets. Allison shot her a panicked look. Millie squeezed Grandma Cooke's hand. "I'll be right back."

She managed to get to the counter before him, rubbing her hands against her jeans, then hiding them beneath her apron. Allison stood behind her, one arm on her wrist as though she were concerned Millie might try to deck the man. Millie tried on a slight smile instead. "I don't think you've been inside the bakery before."

He wasn't tense, but he didn't look like he intended to smile either. "Your window's made quite the buzz. Thought I'd come see."

"Christmas season surprise, didn't want to spoil it."

He looked at the shelves of goods behind the counter. "Are those French krullers? I'll take two. Never thought about painting the window. I'll have to see how yours turns out." He pulled his wallet from his back pocket.

Millie stood for a moment. She hadn't been able to keep a straight face when he walked past after the sign incident. Could he be that cool? Had someone else messed with the window?

"Can I get the donuts?"

She shook herself. "Of course, sorry." She turned, grabbed a bag and a plastic glove. She set the krullers side by side to prevent the iced tops from messing up. She folded the bag and placed it on the counter in front of him. "Four-fifty."

"Four-fifty? Don't you have a neighborhood discount?"

"That is the discount."

He frowned but pulled a five from his wallet and held it out to her. The edge of his white sleeve had a spot of orange. A familiar shade of orange. She took the money as he rubbed at the spot. "Huh, I wonder how that got there." He didn't smile or give anything else away. With a nod, he took the bag. "Thanks."

He turned calmly and walked from the bakery.

Millie watched his back until the front door closed behind him. There was no doubt now, and she needed to come up with a brilliant scheme to get him back.

4

Thanksgiving morning, Stella perused the drawer of glasses to decide which best matched her pumpkin-spice colored dress with fringe. The multi-colored rims on the end included orange. She tried them on, leaning away from the mirror to see herself better. With everything in focus, she tilted her head. Dark wavy hair was pushed behind her ears. The almond-shaped wide rimmed glasses complemented her face. She added a touch of cinnamon lip gloss and darkened her eyebrows.

There were a few hours to enjoy Thanksgiving with family and friends. Then she would help clean up at the bakery because Millie had to start pestering the bookshop owner.

"Almost ready?" Millie called from downstairs. "I got the pies and cookies in the car."

Stella slipped into a pair of tawny ankle boots. "On my way."

She met Millie at the front door. Millie sighed. "I go shopping with you and I still can't put myself together the way you do."

"We each have our talents." Stella hooked arms with her sister. "What kind of cookies did you make?"

"I know I made pumpkin-flavored sugar cookies last year. I mixed a brown sugar cinnamon filling for them this year."

Stella grinned. "Now who's got talent?"

Crisp morning air marked the advent of Thanksgiving Day. Millie parked her blue crossover behind a classic yellow thunderbird. Aunt Bea's house was a warm Victorian craftsman, one of the larger houses a few streets from downtown. The front porch was wide. Wicker rocker pairs on either side of the front door remained as they always had. The yellow door stood out against the lighter blue color and creamy aged trim.

Stella slammed the passenger door. "What do you want me to grab?"

"The cookie trays. I'll get pies from this side."

It didn't take long to be climbing the stairs. Old boards creaked beneath her boots. Stella didn't want it any other way. The front door burst open.

Aunt Lettie held the screen door. She kissed Stella's cheek. "Good morning, dear."

"Morning, Auntie," Millie said. She raised the pecan pie. "We have deserts, of course. Where are we putting them?"

"The buffet in the hallway. Maybe we can keep people out of pumpkin spice pie until after they've had their turkey."

Stella laughed. "Doubtful, but good of you to try."

Stella followed Millie to the hall on the other side of the dining room. They placed the deserts on the buffet. Millie then wrapped an arm around Aunt Lettie. "How can we help?"

"Help?" Aunt Lettie gasped with dramatic flair.

"With this gaggle of uppity middle-aged girls? We aren't dotards yet."

Millie laughed. "Just because we set a table doesn't mean we think you can't."

"Course not, dear." She patted Millie's cheek. "The boys were here early enough to do any menial tasks needing done. You've brought the cherry on top of our Thanksgiving feast. Sit and relax. I'm sure you rarely do."

Stella arched one brow. "We're cleaning up, aren't we?"

"No, you promised last year…" Millie giggled, unable to continue the familiar argument. Aunt Lettie left with a wave.

Stella studied the long wood table that easily sat a dozen guests. Its cherry finish gleamed. Ten places were set with orange placemats, china dishes, silver, and a sprig of herbs tied in a bundle on top of the small bowl. "Who's been watching the home and garden channel?" she called.

Mrs. Mildred followed by her husband, Sanders, entered with a vat of potato salad.

"I love that show," Mrs. Mildred gushed, then asked her husband. "Who are they? You know." She turned back to Millie and continued without waiting for an answer to her question. "Sweetest couple with four children. Or is it five now? She's got style, that one. And I don't mean just her ability to make any old house look like a gem."

Sanders, a tall thin shadow to his pudgy wife, didn't seem to mind not having to respond. They set their dishes on the buffet and headed back to the kitchen.

Stella shook her head. "Good thing he likes to be

quiet and she likes to talk."

"They have good balance."

"Or bad balance that works well."

They walked to the living room. High ceilings, cream walls, and flood of light through tall windows gave the room a light, airy feel. Millie crossed to the lounging side of a sectional and flopped into the corner, curling her feet up beside her. "Ah, a moment to relax."

Stella sat on the other end, tugging an afghan over her legs. "Only a moment. We still have to clean the windows after we finish here."

Millie jumped up. "I wanted to see if that squeegee is under the cabinet in the bathroom."

"Might as well grab a washcloth while you're in there. I can wash the dishes after we eat."

"I'm washing. I call dibs already," Millie declared as she ran from the room.

Stella yelled after her, "I'm not drying this year."

"Get your aunt a dishwasher for Christmas." The unexpected familiar voice had Stella jumping to her feet.

She jerked around and came face to face with her past. "Hugh Granger!" Stella didn't think. She jumped the couch like a hurdle and hugged him. His chest was thicker, arms stronger, possibly even taller, but her high school sweetheart felt familiar.

"Hey, Stells."

"What are you doing here?" She squeezed his arms. "How are you? Where's your wife? I heard you were getting married."

"Whoa. Your nose for news hasn't changed." He tweaked the end of her nose. She stepped back and punched him in the arm. "Ow." He rubbed the spot, an exaggerated look of pain on his face.

"That's for not warning me you were coming home for Thanksgiving." She peaked around him. "Where is she?"

He shrugged. "I didn't get married."

"What? Aunt Lettie told us you were good together. I'm sorry it didn't work out."

He grinned. "We were good, but we mutually decided great options were waiting for us."

Stella frowned. "What's that supposed to mean?"

"We weren't," he tried to explain. "Remember *Sleepless in Seattle*? They were good, but there was a great relationship out there, too. We decided we wanted great."

Stella shook her head. "Then what brings you here?"

"I'm going to sit down and give you exactly twenty questions. Five of which you've already used up."

"Deal." Stella returned to the couch and pushed her boots off. She curled onto the end, leaning against the armrest, facing Hugh.

Hugh sat on the other side, leaning against the back of the couch and straddling his left leg across his right. "You look great, by the way."

"Thanks. You've grown into yourself." Stella grabbed the afghan and leaned over it. "So, tell me, what brings you here?"

"Grandmom started it. They restored Ives mansion and carriage house south of town. The heritage group wants to turn it into a museum. They've hired me to handle acquisitions."

"You can do acquisitions with an archivist degree?"

"That's the second hat they gave me. Organize an

archive of the Ives estate and St. Ives itself."

Stella smirked. "That'll take a lifetime. You're stuck here in the cold."

"Trips to the Caribbean are possible any time of the year."

Stella laughed. "Do you have a house in town?"

"Apartment above the carriage house for now. I'll look for a place eventually. I hear you own a bakery."

"With Millie. She does most of the cooking. I get to take care of the business, enjoy a touch of artistic flair now and then."

He waved at her outfit. "Artistic flair remains a talent of yours."

"Thank you," she did a little bow. "Millie said the same thing."

"Are you seeing anyone?"

"In St. Ives?" She scoffed. "Besides, we've been busy getting the business off the ground. You're the one who almost nabbed himself a wife."

"Living in a big city offers more opportunities to meet people."

"Small towns have survived this long. A man'll come along eventually, right?"

"Like me?"

She grinned. "The women in town who didn't know you as the scrawny teen will be all over you."

Aunt Lettie broke into their tete-a-tete. "Hugh, dear. A couple next door have a pot of mashed potatoes. Can you fetch it for us?" Aunt Lettie leaned over and kissed Stella's cheek. "Happy Thanksgiving."

"Yes, Grandmom."

"Aunt Lettie."

Hugh and Stella spoke at the same time and the

three of them laughed.

Hugh shook his head. "That's right. My grandmother is your Aunt Lettie, and your Grandmother is my Aunt Sylvie. I think we should all stick with first names."

"Get on with you, boy." Aunt Lettie shewed him. "Dinner's waiting." She sat with a grunt beside Stella. "Old bones and cold."

"Make him take you to the Bahamas."

"I don't pay him enough to take me to the Bahamas." She patted Stella's hand. "I meant to warn you he was in town but forgot."

"Why warn me?"

"You dated."

Stella laughed. "In high school. Over a decade ago."

"One never forgets first love." She sighed. "Of course, I married mine. Sweetest man, even when I wanted to kill him."

"I remember. Aren't too many men like Uncle Al and Grandpa Rob."

"God wanted them more than us. Now we have a great circle of friends and a good focus for our attention."

"Who? Your grandkids?"

She slapped Stella's hand. "St. Ives Heritage Club."

"If you ever need help with numbers, feel free to ask."

"You have a degree in accounting, don't you?"

"And business management. Which is good, because Millie doesn't pay attention to much beyond baking."

Aunt Lettie rubbed her stomach. "We know your sister's talents too well. What did she bring for

Thanksgiving?"

Millie knocked on the side of the doorway as she leaned into the room. "Hey, you two. Dinner's set up. You planning to join us?"

Stella stood then helped Aunt Lettie to her feet. "Go ahead, let me get my shoes on." She slipped her feet back into the boots.

Millie waited in the doorway. "You good?"

"Sure."

"Absolutely?"

Stella slapped her arm. "We dated in high school. That's it. You heard he was supposed to get married this past fall."

"But he didn't. He's here alone."

"Won't stay that way. Hugh's a good man and there are way too many single women in this town."

"Of all ages," Aunt Dahlia greeted with a kiss on first Millie, then Stella's cheek. "What's this about Hugh?"

"He won't be single for long." Stella stated.

"Are you setting your cap for him, dear?" Dahlia was every bit as beautiful as the flower she'd been named for. Her shoulder length silver hair had hints of lavender highlights.

"Had my chance at him, Auntie D. Didn't take." It was true. The hurt feelings from high school were gone. Seeing the man Hugh had become felt good.

Heads bowed around the table as Mr. Sanders offered a prayer of Thanksgiving. Millie peeked around the table. Hoary heads came to mind, although from the lavender colors mixed with gray, the hair salon had been busy in the past week. Sanders and Mildred Prince were the two she didn't know very well. Aunt Bea said they lived further down the street. Allison sat beside her brother. Aunt Dahlia and Aunt Bea sat at the ends of the table. She heard the conclusion and lifted her head. "Amen." She turned to Aunt Bea on her right. "What happened to Millicent and her nephew?"

"He surprised her with a Bahama cruise. Not sure what his intent is, but she was happy to pack bags that required a swimsuit and not a parka."

Millie laughed. "That's understandable."

Chairs scooted across the wood floor as people took their plates to get food. "Turkey and ham? How are we to decide?" Hugh grunted.

"We're a family of cooks, that's for sure." Millie joked. "How many kinds of dressing does one Thanksgiving meal need?"

"It's a matter of having choice. We had to have cornbread and giblet. Some people," she looked at Stella, "don't like them together."

Stella shrugged. "I refuse to eat that far into a bird."

"Same ol' Stells," Hugh teased. "I see you're getting sweet potatoes with and without pecans. What's your reason for that?"

"Being polite. Not sure who made them."

Millie elbowed Stella but looked at Hugh. "What did you bring?"

"Rolls." He pointed at the Hawaiian King bag. "Simple, no cooking necessary."

"Shameful." Stella sniffed, but took one of the rolls anyway.

The plates were too full for everything. Cranberries and sweet pickles made their way to the table. Hugh gave Millie and Stella a hopeful look. "Are you girls staying through this evening?"

"Unfortunately, we've work to do at the bakery once we've finished cleaning up here."

"You have enough business to get you to work on Thanksgiving?"

Millie shook her head. "We do have a ton of business from the city. People still prefer bakery goods to what they can buy in a chain grocery store. But no, that's not the problem for today. We have a window to clean up."

"What window? Did you break a window?" Aunt Bea asked.

"The store front, no it isn't broken. Seems we have an artist on the block."

Grandma Cooke frowned. "What did they do to your window? Did you call the police? Do you know who did it?"

Millie rolled her eyes. "We have a suspect but no real proof. I don't think it will be much trouble. More like a prank really."

"But you just had it painted for Christmas."

Stella waved her fork in the air. "On the inside. This was done on the outside."

Grandma Cooke still seemed out of sorts. "More than you should have to put up with."

"Millie started it."

"Did not," Millie protested, tossing a hard look at her sister. "We can't be sure it was him."

"You said he had orange paint on his sleeve."

"Who?" Aunt Bea asked.

"Doesn't matter." Millie tried to distract her aunt. "Who made the cranberry salad? This is delicious."

Hugh groaned. "It all is, isn't it?" He took another bite of mashed potatoes.

Aunt Bea wasn't deterred by the change of topic. "Who do you think trashed the front window?"

Stella plowed ahead. "Owner of the book shop."

"Mr. Dane?" Several of the Widow Peeps looked surprised. Aunt Bea had turkey gravy dripping off her fork. "That nice-looking man?"

Millie grunted. "How can a person look nice if they never smile?"

"He might not have anything to smile about. Once you get to know him, that could change."

"I can safely say I will not get to know Baxter Dane. Ever." Millie pushed stuffing around her plate. "I think I'm ready for pumpkin spice pie."

Aunt Dahlia shook a finger. "Finish your meal, young lady."

Everyone chimed in. "There are starving children in Africa."

The break between dinner and desert allowed Stella and Millie to clear dishes from the table and get the dining dishes washed. Cooking pans were soaking on the counter. Bellows from the den marked the interest in the game. Stella leaned against the doorway. Mr. Sanders and Hugh had the couch. The football whizzed across the TV screen, and the men high fived each other. Grandma Cooke had her feet up on the Laz-y-boy, closer to napping than paying attention to what was on TV. "I guess no need for desert in this room," Stella announced, then laughed as the men jumped to their feet and Grandma Cooke pushed the lever to lower the footrest.

"How many pies do we have?" Hugh asked as he offered his hand to Grandma Cooke.

"Too many." Stella teased.

Mr. Sanders clicked his tongue. "Never too many."

Stella let the men pass through the door, waiting for Grandma Cooke. She linked their arms and walked together into the dining room.

5

Millie thought about her words never to get
to know Baxter Dane as she used the squeegee to wipe
another section of the window. The paint came off with
relative ease. Going up and down the ladder proved
more irritating. That and the chill in the dark air. Stella
waved at her from inside the bakery where she pulled
down sheets of brown paper.

Pity to waste paper. Millie glanced down the empty
street. Nothing bad, just a little message to let him
know that she knew. Millie waved for Stella to come
outside. "Don't wrinkle the paper. I think I'll be able to
reuse it."

"Not on the baking pans."

"Course not. I'll find a different use for them. Lay
them across the island in the kitchen for now."

Stella yawned. "Fine. Finish this and head home."

Millie wiped the final bit of paint from the window.
"You head home. I'll clean up and meet you there."

"Sure?"

"Positive."

"Positively sure?"

"Absolutely." Millie gathered used towels and
dropped them in the trash as she walked into the

bakery. "I want to get a few things set up for tomorrow." She rubbed her stomach with a groan. "Still too full to settle down."

Stella helped her get the ladder in the storeroom before heading home. It was almost eight. Millie rolled the paper to make it easier to carry, then grabbed duct tape and Stella's stool from under the counter.

The street was deserted, and the bookstore was dark save for a light above the book tree in the window. Millie took a sheet of the butcher paper, climbed the stool, and taped the paper to the frame above the door. Two sheets covered the front. That was enough. He would know that she knew. But maybe the back door as well. Millie picked up her supplies and returned to the bakery.

The Christmas scene in the bakery window gleamed. After going inside, she locked the front. The café appeared ready for the next day. With lights out, the exit sign over the door glowed red and a spotlight shone on the logo painted on the wall behind the register. The kitchen was clean as well. It was an easy task to get flour, sugar, and recipes set for morning. She double-checked to be certain the small coffee pot had fresh grounds. When everything was set, she headed out the back door after setting the alarm. As she locked the heavy metal door, she peered down the row of shops. It was darker than up front. She could still tape paper over the back door. The duct tape was on her wrist, the butcher paper under her arm, and the stool held by one of the legs. But it was late, and dark. Where the front held fun, here had a more-sinister edge. Millie headed for her car instead.

6

Millie rarely needed an alarm for four o'clock in the morning. Most mornings, just like today, she sat at the round table in the kitchen enjoying a cup of coffee as she read the newest Guidepost.

Stella turned into the kitchen shortly after four. Today's glasses were pink, and she used a matching headband to hold back her damp curls. "Did you sleep?"

"Soundly. Ready for black Friday madness?"

Stella held her arms up. "I can cook. I can clean. I can minister to our patrons."

Millie gulped the last of the coffee. "May we have more than enough for the two of us."

"Don't forget Angela and Allison will be there by nine."

The drive to the bakery went smoothly. Nothing in St. Ives opened before eight Friday morning. The only vehicle they passed was the laundry truck. "I think our special today should be a baking treat and drink combo," Stella suggested.

Millie used her signal to turn into the parking lot behind the row of shops. "Great idea. Do you want to make the sign?"

Stella shook her head. "Your handwriting is nicer than mine. I'll start the muffins."

"Start with gingerbread and white Christmas."

Millie propped the A-frame sign on one of the café tables before digging beneath the countertop for chalks. Within a few minutes, fall leaves had been cleared away and a wreath of ivy and holly framed the announcement special.

Morning progressed, and Angela arrived with the first customer in tow.

"Good morning, girls," Aunt Lettie called. Millie put the tray of muffins on the counter and greeted the older woman with a hug.

"What brings you downtown today? Angela talk you into serving tables?"

"Ha. Those days are well over, thank the Good Lord. Are those the white chocolate muffins you make?"

She nodded. "First batch comes out on Black Friday. Want a coffee or cocoa with it? It's today's special."

"Perfect. Black coffee please. Get me ready for shopping"

"Are the sales worthwhile this year?"

"Shopping downtown is worthwhile. Much more interesting than department stores that are a dime a dozen."

"Carolers and sleigh rides start this afternoon. Pace yourself. You can enjoy a horse-drawn carriage ride later." Millie placed the coffee and muffin on a table near the front window. She made sure Aunt Lettie settled in her seat and then carried the sign outside.

She peaked down the street. Garland twirled around

the streetlamps. Business fronts with steps and rails had the rails wrapped in garland as well. The brown paper had been removed from the bookstore doorway. Butterflies fluttered. What would he do? And why was she grinning like a schoolgirl? Millie stared at the ground and got the giddy feeling under control. She fixed the sign and went back inside.

The beautiful crisp sunny day brought people in droves. Millie soon forgot her concern with Dane's retribution when baking and serving absorbed her time.

"This is the last batch of White Christmas we can bake today," Stella hollered as she dropped the final scoops of white chocolate chips into the raspberry muffin batter.

"I think our numbers today will be better than anything we've seen in four years."

"Wish I could get outside and enjoy this beautiful weather," Stella groaned as she turned the mixer to low.

"Sunday will come. Pray the weather holds."

Even though most of the retail shops remained open until after dark, there was little point in keeping the bakery open later. Most of their shelves were emptied. The supply truck brought the necessities for Saturday before they would open. They could start again in the morning.

Angela flopped into a chair in the corner of the kitchen. "This would be the perfect place for a jacuzzi."

Stella gave her a cookie. "Long soak in a hot tub is a divine idea."

"Don't forget we've got the light parade tomorrow night. Do whatever you need to rest up tonight. Tomorrow will be another doozy of a day." Millie pulled herself onto the counter, waving her feet back and forth as she kept her hands wrapped around a large warm mug of cocoa.

Angela groaned as she took a bite of the cookie. "I don't know how you girls manage to stay in shape. I'm running extra miles a day."

"Discipline," Stella offered.

"Not," Millie laughed. "We stay too busy to enjoy much of our work. And I'd rather give our leftovers to the shelter in Standish than keep it for myself."

"Is that what you do? I used to worry about finding people rummaging through the trash cans."

"Thankfully not. A few members of the board for Standish Center of Hope attend our church. We made an arrangement with them."

"I hadn't heard anything."

"No need to. Although, days like today make me feel a little bad."

"No, they don't," Stella protested.

Millie laughed. "Very little."

Stella stood and stretched. "I have a date with a couch. Are you picking up dinner, sis?"

"I called an order to Boston Market. About all the energy I have left."

Stella gathered her things to leave as Millie washed the few remaining dished. She heard the back door close, and then open a few moments later.

"Uh, Mills? What did you do with those sheets of butcher paper?"

Millie dried her hands. "Why do you ask?"

"Your car is wrapped up with them."

"What?" Millie frowned.

Allison jumped to her feet. The three women pushed outside. The paper was wrapped around the middle of her crossover. The two sheets she'd taped on the bookstore hadn't gone fully around the vehicle. A wide red ribbon held it in place. There was even a bow on top. Millie jerked to a stop. "That's odd."

"Is it to advertise? I don't get it." Angela walked around the car.

"I didn't do this."

"When would you have time?" Stella agreed.

"Who would waste their time wrapping your car like this?"

"It's probably the bookshop owner." Millie pulled her lips between her teeth to keep from smiling.

"Baxter Dane?" Angela scoffed.

Stella frowned at Millie. "What did you do?"

Millie hated the feel of heat through her cheeks. "I only taped a few sheets of paper across his front door."

"Millicent Imogene."

"That is not worth full name recognition. It's perfectly harmless. When did he have time to do this?"

Angela smacked a bubble of gum. "Better yet, how did no one notice?"

Millie rubbed her chilled arms. "I will take care of it after I put on my coat and grab a pair of scissors."

"If you don't need me, I'm getting my stuff and heading home." Angela speed walked back to the bakery.

Millie turned to go as well, but Stella's firm voice slowed her steps. "We have plenty of work for the holiday season. Now isn't time to keep going back and forth with a neighbor. If a trick on *either* side backfires, it'll hurt our bottom line."

"You're right. It's silly. I can definitely put my energy into more profitable pursuits." Millie agreed.

"Getting dinner and bringing it home is all the pursuit you need today."

7

Saturday night arrived clear and cold. Millie wiggled her wool-encased toes as she watched the lights along Mainstreet turn on. Reds and greens of Christmas glowed through the yellow-toned streetlamps. She held her ceramic mug of hot chocolate, absorbing its warmth through her mittens.

Stella joined her, jostling through the gathered crowd. "It's a busy night for sure." She pushed candy cane colored glasses into place.

"Don't think I've seen this many visitors." An unfamiliar masculine voice added.

Millie turned and felt a jolt to her body. "What are you doing here?" The words blurted out before she could reconsider.

"Freezing along with the rest of you." He motioned to the red mug she held. "Good idea." He blew into his bare hands.

Millie frowned. "Where are your gloves?"

"Left home without them." He shrugged. "Too busy to do anything about it."

"Wouldn't have taken you for a forgetful man."

Dane laughed. "Usually not." He shoved his hands into his pockets. The parade had yet to begin. With a sigh, Millie decided to be helpful. "Would you prefer hot apple cider or hot chocolate?"

"For what?"

"To keep your hands warm during the parade."

"I don't think that's necessary."

Stella butted in with a grunt. "Be polite and accept the offer. Give her a chance to see how it feels to be helpful."

Millie turned her frown to Stella. "Hey."

Dane studied them both, then glanced at the big red mug. "Okay. I'd prefer the cocoa."

Millie turned to Stella. "Save my spot."

Stella grabbed Dane's hand. "We won't let anyone steal your space."

Millie rolled her eyes but moved toward the bakery. The hot chocolate simmered on the stove. She grabbed a heavy green mug and filled it as full as she could safely carry. She plopped a couple of small marshmallows into the mixture, and then refilled her own drink. With her gloves pulled back on, she headed to the front.

The cold outside felt colder after the warm bakery. That's what was making her shiver as Dane's lip twitched into a half-smile. His hands were turning red. "We have oven mitts if you don't mind wearing them." She offered as he took the green mug.

"Ah." His sigh of relief made her stomach flop. "This feels good."

"I see lights, they're coming," Stella yelled as she bounced.

Millie gladly turned her attention to the approaching car draped in white Christmas lights. The driver of the convertible honked, Christmas music blasting from his stereo. The line of classic cars was followed by a stately horse with a flowing mane pulling a large red sleigh with Santa. The jolly elf laughed and waved as green clad helpers brought candy canes to the people watching the parade. Stella cheered when she got one. An elf held one for Millie, but Dane snatched it first.

"That's mine," Millie protested, reaching for her prize.

Dane held it aloft. "He was handing it to me."

"Which is why you had to sneak in and snatch it?"

"Can't help if I'm quicker than you. Tell you what, we can split it."

She narrowed her eyes at him. "You cut; I choose."

Dane laughed, a rich sound that wrapped around Millie. "I haven't heard that since I was twelve. Very well. Hold my mug."

Millie complied, then watched as Dane pressed his fingers on the longer part of the cane. "Move closer to the hook so pieces come out even." She offered help.

"Thought I was cutting and you choosing?"

"Whatever. Just hurry up. I've been waiting to dip my minty candy cane in hot chocolate."

"Lukewarm chocolate by now. But you have a good idea. I haven't put a candy cane in hot chocolate since I was young."

"Next thing I know you'll accuse me of being immature."

He held up both ends of the broken candy cane. "If the shoe fits."

She took the straight piece and gave him back his mug. She used the candy cane to stir her hot chocolate.

More cars drove by, colors flashing from white to green to yellow, and then blue. The melody of Christmas carols filled the air. The final car passed followed by a crowd of people.

"If you can't walk with your mug, you can set it by the door."

"I can manage, I think. If I end up breaking it, I promise to pay you."

"Should I take your credit card details down now?"

"What, don't trust me?"

Millie grinned. "Can't imagine why not."

"Are you two coming?" Stella grabbed Millie's arm.

"Well, I am. I have no idea what he's planning to do."

Dane kept up with them, surprising Millie. Stella led them closer to the tall tree in the town square.

"Your sister must really want a good spot," Dane teased, grabbing hold of Millie's coat sleeve as Stella pulled them through the crowd.

"Dane, you made it to the festivities."

Millie turned at the sultry voice.

"Nora." Dane greeted. "How are you?"

"Much better now, thank you." Nora peeked around him. "Hello, Millicent."

Millie pasted a smile on her face. Nora was the only woman in the world who called Millie by her full name. Had since fifth grade when Nora learned Millie hated it. "Good evening, Nora."

Nora placed a hand on Dane's arm. "Did you bring Irish coffee? With or without the coffee?" Her teetering laugh still annoyed.

"They're getting ready to light the tree," Stella declared, jumping. The crowd counted backward from five. After one, the tree blazed into its Christmas glory. White and blue lights wrapped the tree from its pinnacle to its trunk. Large wrapped packages beneath the tree also glowed. "Beautiful," Stella gasped.

"Could have gotten a better tree from upstate New York," Nora grumbled.

"This one's good. It fits the space," Dane disagreed. Nora latched onto his arm once more.

"You're a man. You don't notice details the way we do." She glanced around. "Well, I do." She tossed her hair with a shake of her head, sending a humorless smile toward Millie.

Stella pushed on her glasses. "Stout's farm has provided our Christmas tree for a hundred years. Nothing in upstate New York is better than local."

"Simple charming girls, aren't they? How's the bakery? I hope Dane's cookies aren't impacting your sales. Have you tasted them?" She closed her eyes. "Divine."

Millie straightened as she fought weariness. "I'm sure they are. It's been a long day. I think I'm ready to go."

"The hours a baker keeps," Nora shook her head. "How do you do it?" She turned to Dane. "You don't have to leave, do you?" She tilted her head upward and batted her eyes.

Did men fall for that? They must. Dane was gazing down on Nora's slender face. Millie felt an urge to throttle him and slam her boot down on Nora's foot. "I'll take the mug." She grabbed it from him before he could respond. Cooled chocolate splashed over her mittens, but she ignored it. "Ready, Stella?"

"Sure." Stella blinked, watching the three of them.

Millie walked away, but she could still hear Nora.

"Your hands are bare; you must be freezing."

What would he do? Probably let Nora pull his hands into her pockets. Irritation nibbled between Millie's shoulders. Ridiculous.

8

Millie wanted to kick herself for letting her mind wander to the bookstore. Again. It was the first Tuesday of the Christmas season. She needed to focus on the cake covered with gray fondant and white snowflakes. The sophisticated three-layer white cake with chocolate crème would be the centerpiece of the winter gala. It took both hands to add the pearls, but the final product looked amazing. Millie leaned back in her artist's stool to admire the masterpiece.

Stella breezed past. "Cookies aren't as showy, but they still need to be cooked."

"What have you been doing?" Millie asked as she checked the cake box against the actual size of the cake. Big enough to fit the pedestal, good. Stella disappeared by the time Millie placed the boxed-up cake in the walk-in fridge. Fatigue tugged, but she pulled the floor mixer to the long island. In a matter of minutes, the ingredients for brownie crispers spread across the island countertop. She took a minute to switch the radio channel on her phone to a Christmas station, then started the mixer. Humming the *Night before Christmas* turned to belting *Deck the Halls*. Before long, she was plopping bite-size rolls of dough onto cookie sheets.

The oven dinged the perfect temperature. Millie set four pans evenly spaced in the baker's oven. The mess remained, but with a sigh, she sat at the counter, pressing the timer on her phone. Music faded, and she dropped her head on her arms, waiting for the timer to go off.

She fell asleep instead. An acrid smell tickled her nose. As the scent of burning registered, she jumped to her feet. The stool crashed back. Faint plumes of smoke rose from the oven vent. With a cry, Millie ran to the oven and turned it off. Her mistake was opening the oven door. Plumes turned into a cloud. The mitts were still on the counter. She raced across the room as an alarm overhead started chiming.

She threw on a mitt, grabbed the top pan, and ran for the back door. Cold blew into the kitchen, helping disperse smoke. She dropped the pan outside and ran to get the next. Smoke was thinner. She waved the other oven mitt at the sensor and the alarm silenced. She sighed with relief. Another minute and the four pans lay against the side of the building. The ruined brownie crisps looked more like dog refuse.

Millie slumped against the open doorway, rubbing the back of her neck. She swatted at something flying toward her face, but it wasn't a bug. Puffs of snow were falling. The first few flurries were soon overtaken by larger, thicker flakes. Several landed on burnt cookies, the stark white contrasting with the brown.

An evil thought came to mind, and she tried to ignore it. Stella was right, Christmas season wasn't the time to engage in childish pranks with a neighbor. Perhaps the snow wouldn't last or even stick. The chill in the air had her returning to the kitchen. Closing the door, she intended to clean up the kitchen and head home. She could start fresh in the morning. An empty plastic bin with a lid nabbed her attention. She shouldn't. She really, really shouldn't. But there were other reasons to keep the burnt cookies. Tax purposes for ruined inventory? She grabbed the bucket, returned to the outdoors, and gathered the burnt cookies. She pressed the sides of the bucket firmly, locking the lid in place. She took it to the freezer, finding a bare corner to store the container. Just in case.

By the time she finished cleaning the kitchen, any semblance of weariness had gone. Excitement stirred as she gathered her coat and purse. Delight made her want to giggle as she opened the back door and stepped outside. A thin layer of snow covered the industrial trashcans and the few cars remaining in the back lot. The snow was sticking.

9

Dane scrapped the slim pile of snow away
from the rear entrance to The Book Shop. The blanket
of white on this crisp, cold midmorning was enough to
add Christmas ambiance to the town, not enough to
keep shoppers away. After stomping his feet on the
commercial-grade carpet just inside the shop, he turned
to the right to deposit his laptop on his desk. He
continued down the hall. The switch to the back room
on the left was beside the doorway. He turned on the
lights. Leather back chairs were set around a
rectangular wood table. The orange padded armchair
had a magazine laying across one of its arms. Exactly
as it should be.

He moved to the next room. The old-fashioned
fireplace with its rounded hood worked on gas. He
pressed the button and set the flames low, encouraging
an orange-red glow among the gas logs. He moved the
barrier screen into place. The set of gold-leaf patterned
burgundy armchairs were far enough away. The heat
from the fireplace should not be uncomfortable. He
arranged the pillow on one of the chairs and then
crossed through the arched doorway into the front
room.

The table in the bay window had the book tree dressed in garland and a variety of angel figurines. He pushed a pudgy cherub from the edge as he went to the grandfather clock hanging on the wall between the bay window and a double-hung flat window. He took the key from its spot and wound the clock after checking his wristwatch for the correct time. He fixed the clock, pushed the weight, and waited for the repeating tick-tock before closing the front face of the clock.

He walked to the narrow table set beneath the normal window and pulled out the box beneath it. Napkins, sweeteners, stirrers, a honey pot and cinnamon shaker were set in place. He crossed the hallway, unlocked the front shop door and flipped the neon sign open as he made his way to the rooms on the other side of the main door. The second front room was a mirror image in shape, although the arrangement was intended for children, not adults. He passed the children's section to get to the work room in the back. Cream and milk from the fridge were poured into labeled thermoses. He returned to the serving table in the front, placing the milks on the table. As he glanced through the window, he noticed a figure scurry to the far side of the sidewalk as they passed the bookstore.

Dane frowned. He moved to the bay window and leaned over. Hadn't they shoveled the in front of the store steps? The mound of snow by the window suggested they had. He noticed a dark object in snow. Had someone dropped something?

He went to the front door, opening it. His mouth dropped at the sight. A pack of dogs had used his front stoop as their poop deck. The snow around the door had been stained yellow and brown. Evidence from the dogs stuck up in places.

His stomach turned, and he swallowed the urge to bring up breakfast. Who let their dogs…? He was turning back into the shop to try to find supplies to clean up the mess, when a thought made him pause. He turned back around, wrinkling his nose at the nasty— where were the paw prints? If there had been that many dogs, and from the amount of waste in the snow there must have been several, where were the scrapes and tracks of dog feet? In fact, what few tracks there were appeared more human than animal.

She didn't. Dane knelt, pulling a pen from his pocket. He jabbed at the nearest blob of brown. Instead of what he expected, the thing moved. He tapped it. It was hard. This close, he could smell burnt chocolate.

That little… he looked up the block. But there was nobody to be seen in the bakery. He grinned, and then rubbed his hand across his face. He was not amused, he tried to convince himself, and there was nothing clever about the stocky baker.

Okay, she wasn't stocky.

Millie couldn't bear to wait to witness the fruits of her labor. Before lunch, she grabbed the broom as an excuse to head outside. Most of the snow had turned to slush. The broom didn't offer much help clearing the few areas of the front stoop.

She looked down the sidewalk. Dane crouched beside the stairs to his bookshop. He didn't wear a jacket, even though temperatures hovered near thirty-five. Instead, he dropped his arm into a bucket and pulled out a dripping wet scrub brush.

Millie made a half-hearted attempt at sweeping the sidewalk, looking down and brushing hair behind her ear. She peaked at Dane scrubbing the step. Guilt swept through her. She returned to the bakery kitchen. There was plenty to do. The stack of orders for weekend holiday parties had been separated by type. She tackled the first batch.

But it didn't matter how many chocolate chip whorls she baked; the guilty feel remained. The dye shouldn't have stained anything. The snow had been deep and the stuff washable. Burnt brownies certainly wouldn't, unless someone accidentally stepped on one and ground it into the sidewalk.

Stella bumped against her. "Earth to Millie."

Millie jumped, splattering flour from her dough-caked fingers.

Stella protested. "This is a Ricki original. I wasn't planning to cook today."

Their cousin had a talent for creating dresses in classic designs with a new twist. Stella's dress tied at a high waist and flared to her knees. A darker ruffle of tulle helped the skirt keep its shape. Millie moved her hand to brush at the fleck of flour on the brown top, but Stella backed up. "What's wrong?"

"Nothing's wrong." Millie returned to working the ginger dough.

"You have that furrow right here," Stella pointed at a spot between her eyes.

Millie rubbed her forehead. "I do not." Millie rolled her eyes as Stella stared silently. She caved. "It was a harmless prank."

"What do you mean, prank?" Stella narrowed her eyes. "You didn't."

But Millie nodded. "I burnt a few cookie bites last night."

Stella wrinkled her nose. "That explains the lingering smell."

"I had to dump them in the snow, the alarm was going off." Millie looked down as she pressed through the dough with both hands, turning the sides together and pressing it flat once more. "They looked like... well, you know. The idea just came to me."

Stella frowned. "You dumped burnt cookies around the bookstore?"

Millie giggled. "Looked more like dogs dumped brownies there."

Stella's eyes widened, and Millie bit her lip, reaching for the rolling pin.

"Millicent Imogene, you agreed." Stella glared, hands on hips. "I'm surprised he hasn't stormed in here demanding we clean up your mess."

She grimaced. "He was out this morning scrubbing the sidewalk."

"What?"

"I saw him while I was sweeping the front."

"You never sweep the front walk."

"Felt like a good time to start." Millie eyed the thickness of the rolled dough.

"You need to apologize and make up for it. What if he tries something back? I am not spending another afternoon covering up your escapade."

"You don't have to be mean. I already feel terrible. He didn't even have a jacket on."

"But it's cold outside. He could get sick." Stella stepped closer. "It would be all your fault."

"I'm sending a plate of cookies." Millie pointed at the silver tray with a stack of whorls.

"You should go in person."

LAURIE BOULDEN

She shook her head. "He doesn't like me. You should go. Tell him I apologize, and I'll not come up with anything else." The cookie cutter made a round cookie with a manger scene. Millie greased the cutter and worked her way across the rolled batter.

Stella moved a full tray and set an empty one in its place. "You go. Assure him this is over and ask how you can make it up to him. Be nice."

With the cookies done, Millie had no more excuses to not take the peace offering to The Book Shop. Butterflies in her stomach whipped furiously as she slid her arms into her puffed coat and wrapped a mauve scarf around her neck and head, covering her ears. The matching mittens kept her fingers warm as she stepped into the brisk afternoon. The sun was heading west, and the cold hadn't faded throughout the day. The other store was less than two-hundred feet. She probably didn't need to dress like an Eskimo. She stopped at the bottom of the stairs. There weren't any lingering colors in the snow or discoloration in the cleared steps. Good, no lasting damage. She pulled herself up the steps and entered the store.

A bell rang overhead. It looked like entering a house, with two large rooms on either side of the entry hall. The light was golden. Instead of the rows of dusty shelves with old, worthless books she'd imagined, the shop had a cozy, home feel. The room on the left had three tables. A large one in the middle, then two smaller around it. The right side was a blur of color. Giggling children flopped onto an emerald bean bag beside a fake fireplace.

"Can I help you?" Dane's voice startled her.

She jerked around, nearly losing the plate of

goodies. He managed to grab one end of the platter though she kept hold of the other end.

"Sorry," he smiled. "Didn't mean to…"

The smile unnerved her. It was real, showing up in his eyes. The sparkle pushed what she was meaning to say out of her thought. She realized the moment he recognized her. The smile went away, but oddly, the sparkle in his eyes was still there.

"It's you," he said. He held on to the platter.

"I'm Millie."

"I have a few other names for you."

"You aren't sick, are you? Not getting a cold? Feeling okay?"

"I'm fine." He was puzzled and spoke slowly. "Why shouldn't I be?"

"You were outside without a coat this morning, and its cold."

"I'm a grown man, I can take care of myself."

Millie huffed. Was it hot in there, or was it her?

"We're blocking the front door. Were you coming in? This smells better than your previous delivery."

"What? Oh, yes. These are for you." She allowed him to take the plate. Where was her head? "I don't understand," she spoke to herself, "I'm not usually the dingy one."

"The dingy one?" Dane questioned

Millie unwrapped her scarf. "Stella's not dingy, just not always there."

"Why are you here?"

Millie wrapped her arms around the scarf, holding it against her chest. "To apologize?"

"This should be good." He motioned her to the left.

Millie dropped the scarf on the edge of the big table

and then pulled off her mittens. She closed her eyes and took a deep breath. Upon opening, she noticed his deep blue gaze. "Okay. I'm sorry. The thing with the burnt cookies up front was bad taste." She cracked a smile. "Literally and figuratively, I guess. I certainly did not intend for the sidewalk or stairs to get stained. I felt awful watching you have to scrub."

"Took you long enough to come outside. I thought I was going to freeze."

"I mean the whole painted window things was pretty bad, but," she tilted her head. "What did you say?"

"I waited half an hour for you to come outside. And the water was hot. There was no way I was sticking my hand into a bucket of cold water."

"You weren't scrubbing? You didn't need to scrub?"

"You missed the real clean up and I knew it wouldn't be too long before you had to check on me." he shrugged.

"You faked it." Millie felt the weight in her chest fall away. "I've been worried for hours, and you've been having fun at my expense."

"What's this?" He ignored her, lifting part of the aluminum foil covering on the platter instead.

Millie slapped his hand. "I'm not sure you deserve these."

"They're here, smelling delicious. Might as well show me what I've been missing."

"Fine." She let him pull off the top. The consistency of ginger sugar dough kept the imprint from the cookie cutter sharp. Each cookie had its own magically crisp manger scene. The whorls were chocolate chip cookies, but instead of chips being throughout the dough, she'd layered them into a swirl.

Dane took a chocolate chip cookie first. He hadn't finished what was in his mouth before he was groaning with delight. "Delicious. How do you make cookies taste this good? It tastes the way chocolate chip cookies should taste, but rarely do."

"Thank you." Millie held up her hand to stop his gushing. He'd make her blush. "I really am sorry. I promise not to do anything else. Please, if you're planning more tricks, don't."

He sniffed at the ginger cookie after rubbing his finger across the picture. "Reminds me of Sonji's over in Barkersville."

"Please?" Millie felt her usual calm restoring itself. She would not be distracted.

"One condition."

"What?"

"Help with Monday's reading session. A preschool will be here, and Mrs. Jenkins is going out of town."

Millie frowned. "You want me to read to kids?"

"Yes. On Monday. Nine a.m."

"I've never done that before." What was she supposed to read to a bunch of kids?

"You can read, right?"

"Of course, I can. I'm a baker, that requires reading recipes and ingredients. And lots of other stuff." She straightened. Why would he think she couldn't read?

"Reading to kids is no different than reading to yourself. Come read on Monday, and any thought of retaliation," he wiped his fingers across his forehead.

"Fine. We aren't open, so I'll read Monday." What book did she have to read to preschoolers? "What do I wear?"

His brows rose slightly, and he gave her an evasive shrug. "You always look—what you wear is good. Decent proper. I've never not seen you look proper."

"Okay. Good to know." She grabbed her scarf and gloves. "You can send the platter back later." Why would knowing he paid attention to what she wore make the butterflies swirl through her stomach again? She spun around and rushed for the door.

"I'll see you Monday," he called.

Millie waved without looking back. "Great." She didn't bother putting her scarf or mittens back on. Nor did she notice the nip of cold in the air as she walked back to the bakery.

10

The bookcase in the office of the cottage she shared with Stella offered Millie fewer options of books to read to children than the kitchen shelf. She settled on the cookbook her mother got her in elementary school. The directions included lots of pictures. Children should understand what was happening.

She curled up on the beige easy chair wrapped in a red and green checkered throw blanket. She meant to practice reading aloud once Stella had gone to bed, but the gentle crackle of the fire lulled her to sleep. The alarm jingle on her phone pulled her from a dream. Hitting the snooze button didn't offer enough time to return to her dream, and on the third buzz, she turned the alarm off. A tight stretch knocked the recipe book to the floor. Millie frowned, then look at her phone. Barely enough time to shower, dress, breakfast, and hurry to town. She jumped up, nearly tripping in the afghan wrapped around her. She struggled to pull it off, and then headed for her shower.

A cluster of short people beat her to the shop. She tightened her grip on her purse and shook as little bodies twirled through the hallway.

"Good morning," Dane greeted, corralling the

children into the children's section. "You can set your things in the big chair."

Millie touched the velvet fabric of the giant red chair set in a corner of the children's room. A bookcase lining the wall had circular cutouts for children to sit and lounge as they browsed.

"What's this?" Dane picked up the recipe book she'd set on the seat.

"I'm going to read it to them."

He gave her an odd look. "It's a recipe book."

"I'm a baker. It's the closest thing I have to a children's book at my house."

Dane waved at the room around them. "I own a bookstore."

She followed his wave and glanced at the shelves of books. "How do I pick?"

He walked to a wood Christmas tree shelf and picked up a picture book. "Read this."

An image of a train filled the front cover. 'I've heard of this. It's a movie."

"Based on the book. I'll get the kids on the rug."

Millie didn't have time to read through the story before she was standing in front of a dozen young faces looking up at her. One familiar girl gave a wave. It was the princess birthday cake girl. She waved back.

Dane watched Millie's shoulders relax and a genuine smile brighten her face. With her hair down around her face, she looked pretty. That was not the thought he needed. They might not be enemies, but they weren't going to become anything else.

She opened the book and started to read. Where Mrs. Jenkins could read and show the illustrations at the same time, Millie read and then waved the book at the children too fast. He grabbed a book from the shelf beside him and waited for one of her surreptitious glances to nab her attention. Thought the children did not see him standing behind them, he demonstrated how to pan slowly, allowing time for the illustrations to be enjoyed.

It worked. The next picture, she held the book steady and moved from one side of the room to the other. She glanced at him, and then smiled at his thumbs up.

A few minutes later, quiet of the attentive children changed. As their chatter increased, Dane checked on Millie. She stood in front of the group but appeared to be reading the book to herself instead of the kids. Was she doing it on purpose? He tapped down on the urge to pull the book from her hands. She probably wanted a scene. Instead, he moved toward the Mad Hatter's chair, making an opportunity to whisper to her as he passed. "You're supposed to read to the kids, not for them."

"Oh, my goodness," she jumped. "This is a good story. I forgot to keep reading it to you." A few children laughed. Millie corrected herself, managing to finish without any further distractions. Had it been on purpose or did she have no clue how to read a story to children?

When the story ended, she helped several children climb into the huge chair as the others worked their way into coats and gloves and hats.

"Bennie's going to have himself a new hat if a child doesn't claim this one fast," Dane called out.

With a squeal, the last girl jumped from the chair and reached to pull her pink and white cap from the head of a bear. Dane made to pull it off her head, but she tugged down around her ears and squealed again as she ran to her teacher.

A moment after the front door closed, calm permeated the bookstore. "Wow." Millie stood beside the chair.

"Hard to believe the amount of energy we had at that age," he laughed with her.

"Yet they manage to sit and listen to a story." She tossed her head. "As long as someone remembers to read aloud and not get caught up in the story themselves." She paused, then asked, "Did I do okay?"

Dane wasn't an expert, but she seemed sincere. Any thought she purposefully sabotaged reading time for the kids faded. "You did great. They liked you."

She scoffed. "I wouldn't go that far."

"I think you've at least earned a treat. Come on, you can have a cookie. And do you prefer tea, cocoa, or coffee?"

"Cocoa, of course. Especially if you have the big marshmallows."

"Best way to top off hot chocolate."

"I know, that's one of my signature winter drinks."

Dane changed the carton on the Keurig machine and placed a ceramic coffee mug on the tray. "Are your cups light brown with darker pine trees around it?"

Millie nodded.

He nodded. "I saw a customer carrying their hot chocolate with the lid off. There were marshmallows bobbing, and it reminded me of the bag mom kept in the closet all winter long. What kind of cookie do you prefer?" He tipped over a shallow basket. "Looks like peanut butter or oatmeal raisin."

"Peanut butter."

He set the steaming hot chocolate on a coaster and offered the bag of cookies. When his own drink was ready, he sat across from her at the table. "How's the cookie?" He noticed she'd taken a bite.

"It's okay." Her eyes scooted to the side.

He chuckled. "I know, not bad, but not great. My niece is trying, but she needs a cook like you to teach her what's missing."

"Your niece?"

He nodded. "Her friend is sick. Leukemia. Looks like she'll make it, but Becky is trying to raise money to help the family.

Millie felt horrible. The glee she experienced finding the cookies too bland zipped into guilt. "That's terrible." Millie gasped. "I mean, wonderful of your niece, but how awful for the girl and her family."

"It took a while to convince me, but who can say no to the battle against cancer?"

"Would your niece want baking lessons? I wouldn't want her to feel bad."

"She knows her cookies are only okay. Are you sure? I didn't mean to put you on the spot."

She grinned. "I'll do better with a baking lesson than reading to kids."

"Sure about that? Seems you have a propensity to burn cookies."

"Very funny." Millie stood. "I do need to get going."

"You're closed today."

"The store is closed. I still have orders to fill. Stella's meeting me at noon."

"Take your cocoa with you. I'll get the mug when I return your silver platter."

LAURIE BOULDEN

11

"Ready for our first Christmas holiday weekend. I think this is the final box." Stella taped the lid down and wrote the order name and number on the front. Boxes were stacked four high and three deep across the counter.

Millie stretched before tugging on the trash liner. "People must be gearing up for company parties." She tied the bag securely. "I'll take the trash out if you start those dishes."

Stella agreed. Millie pulled the rolling can through the back door. She was a few feet from the dumpster when a low growl caused her to stop. The night was calm and cold. Maybe she'd heard the wheel on the trash can squeak. She moved forward, and the growl came again. She left the can where it was and ran back to the bakery.

"Where's the flashlight?" She hollered as she grabbed her coat.

"Flashlight for what?" Stella dried her hands on her apron.

"There's a dog by the dumpster. Do we have anything it can eat?"

"Don't feed stray dogs."

"But it might be hurt. And if it stays out there all

night, the cold will kill it."

Stella shook her head. "The thing is probably gone by now." She shuffled through a deep drawer. "Here's the light."

They both went outside. Millie turned on the flashlight and pointed it at the dumpster. There was more growling. "See? He's still here. Did you bring food?"

Stella held up a small bag. "I didn't eat my sandwich. There's roast beef on it."

Millie pulled apart the bread and grabbed a piece of meat. She slowly moved closer, pausing each time the growls started. When she was a few feet, she crouched down and tossed the piece of roast beef at the shadowy paws she could see in the beam from the flashlight. The dog stretched forward but wasn't quite close enough to reach the treat. He scooted.

"Hey there, fellow." Millie called as he sniffed the meat and then gulped it down. She pulled another piece from the sandwich and tossed it to him. He scooted on his belly and gobbled up the second piece as well. "Are you okay? It's cold to be out here by yourself. Wouldn't you rather go home? Are you lost?" She kept talking softly. Next, she pulled a slice of bread, tearing it off and holding it toward him. He crawled forward, tail thumping on the ground, and ate from her hand. "You're a friendly dog, aren't you, sweetheart?"

He was a mid-sized terrier with wiry golden hair. His ears flopped as he sneezed. "Poor sweetheart," Millie cooed. "Do you want to come in with us?"

He sniffed her fingers and gave a lick. Millie scooped him up, placing him against her chest and wrapping her coat around him. He didn't mind. His head poked out at the top and he licked her chin.

"What are you doing?" Stella grabbed the flashlight.

"He's cold."

"He could bite you."

They walked into the kitchen. Millie turned to her sister. "Look at this face. Do you think he'll bite?"

Stella scratched between his ears and he nipped at the bracelet she wore. "Apparently he does. He's young, must have gotten out of his house."

"Or a Scrooge dumped him."

"You and bookstore man stopped your tricks, right?"

"He wouldn't. If a health inspector found a dog hanging around the bakery, we'd be in trouble." Millie studied the dog's bright eyes. "Do you know Dane?" There was a single bark and he licked her nose. She looked at Stella. "Does that mean yes or no? Maybe it's his dog. I should find out."

"He wouldn't be there this late."

"Lights were still on. I saw when I was taking out the trash."

"Why, exactly, are you paying attention to the bookstore?"

Millie shifted the dog and ignored her sister's question. "I'll be right back."

"Better. We've got to clean up and you haven't dumped the trash yet."

Ignoring her sister, Millie escaped through the back door and headed for Dane's. It was his dog, or he planted the dog to cause trouble. Had he been watching her try to entice the dog from his hiding spot?

She knocked on the back door. A moment later, she banged a few times. The dog shivered in her arms. "It's okay," she reassured as she heard a bolt moving. Dane opened the door.

He seemed surprised to see her. "What are you doing here?"

"Are you missing a dog? Or did you dump one by the trash?"

"What are you talking about?"

"We found him by the dumpster."

"Found who?"

She jiggled the dog in her arms.

"The dog?" His forehead scrunched.

"Yes. This little sweetheart."

He opened his mouth but took a few moments before speaking. Red blazed along his cheeks. "It is not my dog, and I would never dump a dog anywhere let alone in a parking lot on a cold day."

Of course, he wouldn't. Why had she allowed the thought to take hold? "If not you, did you see?" His arms crossed, and a vein beat above his right eye causing Millie to swallow and start over. "I mean not you. You wouldn't, I know. I didn't mean to imply you would. But did you see anyone dump him?"

"I would have gotten him if I did. It's too cold outside for a dog to survive." He spoke slow and steady.

Millie got the sense she needed to backtrack quick. "Any customers coming in to ask about a missing dog? From the neighborhood behind us? We didn't have anyone, but maybe you?"

"I can't even see him." He backed up a step. "If you're done thinking I had something to do with this, come in. If you still think I'd harm an animal, you know where the bakery is."

She stepped inside, scooting against the hall wall. He closed the door. "You aren't usually here this late."

"I'm putting out inventory for a hopefully busy Christmas shopper weekend. Let's see him." He waved for her to go into the storeroom.

He didn't smile and kept his distance. Millie placed the dog on the table. The dog sat, wagging his tail and looking at them both. She rubbed her hand against the dog's ear, and it licked her fingers. She glanced at Dane. "I didn't mean to accuse you."

"I would never injure an animal, or worse, to play a prank."

"I know." The way she jumped to conclusions, she'd spend a lifetime apologizing to the man. "Do you recognize him?"

"Unfortunately, no." Dane rubbed the dog's head.

"Then I have a favor to ask. I need to help Stella clean up the bakery, but we can't have a dog in the building."

His laugh was not humorous, "You want me to take the dog."

"Babysit. I mean watch until we're through. You said you're working on inventory."

Dane's fist clenched with the urge to throttle. "First, you accuse me of abandoning the dog and then you want me to take care of it?"

"I didn't mean…" She took a breath, "I get disconcerted around you. I didn't intend to insult you."

"Yet, you did."

She glanced down the street. "You're right, I have no business asking you to watch him. It's late. What health inspector's going to be out now? Anyway, we just found him. Not like we can leave him outside."

"What about tomorrow?"

"What?" Her attention returned to him.

Why did her eyes have to be a pretty, hazel color? He repeated himself. "What will you do with him tomorrow?"

"He'll stay at the house until we find his owner." She scratched between his ears. "He's too cute to be dumped."

Hadn't she just accused him of that dastardly deed? He should be quiet and let her find out the hard way what happens with puppies left home on their own. "Have you ever had a dog?"

She shook her head. "I'm pretty sure Stella and I can figure it out."

Sure, they could. "Dogs don't do well by themselves for long periods of time." What was he thinking? Before he could even consider the fresh thought running through his head, he spoke. "I've kept a dog in the shop. It's easy to cordon off a section. For a day or two only. That should give us time to find the rightful owners."

She frowned, obviously as surprised as himself. "You'd let him stay here during the day? Even after I accused you of dumping him on purpose?"

"I expect you to walk him when you can. And clean up any messes he makes."

"Thank you. That's, uh, nice of you." She seemed as bewildered as he felt. "I should get going. We'll see you tomorrow. If you're sure."

"It'll be fine. I'll see you in the morning." What was he thinking? Another dog at the bookstore? Dane rubbed his hand through his hair. How could a woman infuriate him one moment and make him want to pull her close in a hug the next? Millie of Bake-n-Cake was trouble. What he needed was a lot less, not more, time with her.

Luna the dog didn't seem to mind the bakery. She—Millie was the first to notice it was a she dog—sniffed at the corners of each cabinet. She pulled a hand towel from the handle of the oven, carted it to a corner, and curled up with it. Millie watched from the sink area with one hand holding the industrial spray nozzle.

"I don't like this role-reversal thing." Stella pointed between the two of them. "I get to be the spacy one, not you."

"He offered to watch her the next couple of days. Why would he do that?" Millie moved the faucet over the pile of dishes, filling the tub with water and soap. Bubbles floated into the air as she reached for a pot to clean.

"Must be one of those love hate relationships." Stella teased as she brought another load to the sink.

Millie scoffed. "Baxter Dane never paid me attention, or me him. There was nothing to love or hate."

"That bothered you, didn't it? Isn't that why you started the pranks? To get his attention?"

"He started it, not me. Besides, the initial suggestion to change the sign came from you." Millie pointed a dripping spatula at her sister.

Stella held up her hands. "Only because you asked for ideas."

Millie swung her arm. Soap on the spatula flew at Stella. Stella shrieked, backing away. Luna jumped to her feet, barking excitedly as she chased after Stella. Millie cheered her on. "That's right, girl. You get my evil sister."

"Don't listen to her, Luna." Stella grabbed the jumping dog. "Millicent doesn't know what to make of falling in love."

"I am not falling in love," Millie swore, jabbing the spatula in the bleach solution before setting it on the rack to dry. She pulled up the next pan.

Millie turned over in bed, throwing a pillow over her head, but the dog howling from the bathroom didn't lessen. She sat up with a whimper. "Are you supposed to let dogs sleep in the room with you?" There was no one to answer. It was after midnight. Her four-a.m. alarm loomed. With a sigh, Millie dragged herself from the bed. "I can't regret this any more than I already do." She padded down the hallway in her bare feet, clenching her toes against the chill of hardwood. She opened the bathroom door. Luna sat on her haunches and looked at Millie, the dog head tilting. "What?" Millie whispered. The tail swooshed. Millie leaned down and picked her up. She looked her straight in the eye. "It's almost Friday morning. I need my beauty sleep." Luna licked Millie's chin and rested her head against her neck. Millie sighed. "No messes in my bed, and don't tell Stells." She returned to her bed. Luna curled up on the pillow. With a sigh of relief, they both drifted off to sleep.

The alarm jangled, and then a high-pierced yapping had Millie jumping up in bed. Her hand shook as she swiped her phone to turn off the alarm. She pulled the bob on the bedside lamp, then glared at Luna. The dog blinked, settled on the pillow, and went back to sleep. "Brat." Millie stretched. "Either we're finding your owner or you're changing some habits," she muttered, then dragged herself to the bathroom for a hot shower.

By the time Millie returned from showering, Luna sniffed around a corner of the bedroom. "No, no, no." Millie ran to pick up the puppy. "Not here, you don't. Potty is outside." She hurried downstairs and took Luna through the back door to the small fenced yard. She placed her on the ground and danced as cold wrapped around her. Luna sniffed some more, squatted for a moment, then ran toward the back. "Where are you going?" Millie whispered. The hush of night hung around them. she reached through the door to flip on the porch light. Luna's golden curls could be seen along the fence. Millie rubbed her arms. "Come on, Luna. Come on, girl."

The puppy squatted again, scratched her back legs through the dirt, then bounded toward Mille. Millie grinned. "That's a lot of energy." She picked up the dog and gratefully returned to the warmth of the kitchen. Luna jumped around the legs of the chairs beneath the kitchen table as Millie fixed a cup of tea. After a quick sip, she measured half a cup of puppy food into a bowl and set it on the floor. Luna gobbled then sat, looking at Millie with a silly grin on her face.

Millie shook her head. "I read the label. Half a cup now and half tonight." Luna's look didn't change, which caused Millie to frown. "You probably didn't have much to eat yesterday. Who knows how things were for you before that? Not that you look scrawny."

Luna's tail thumped as Millie talked. Relenting, Millie retrieved another portion of breakfast for the dog. Luna ate with enthusiasm.

"Good morning, Curly." Stella greeted the puppy. Luna bounded across the room then rolled on Stella's feet. She laughed. "Yeah, that's grace." Stella accepted a mug of coffee from Millie. "I talked with Aunt Bea. We can droop Luna at her place. She'll bring her over at nine when she meets up with the Widow Peeps."

"Sure she doesn't want to watch her all day?" Millie asked with hope.

"That could be as bad as having her here all day. At least at the bookstore, someone's there to watch over her full time."

Millie groaned. "We'll see. Not sure I want to owe Dane such a huge favor." Which did not account for the butterflies whirling within her.

Stella smiled. "Be ready for a break when Aunt Bea gets to the bakery. We're better off not letting the dog hang out near food."

Which meant at five till nine, Millie walked to the front display to add a tray of peppermint meringue kisses. When she stood, her heart jolted in her chest. Dane stood in the window. His shoulders and head were above the snowy hill painted on the window. Millie blinked, and his lips thinned in a semblance of a smile. It was easier to smile in return. Aunt Bea drew next to him. Although she couldn't see her aunt, she recognized the Russian-esque winter hat. Luna had arrived. Millie hurried to the door. Cold whipped into her. She waved, "Let me grab my coat and I'll bring her down."

Dane took hold of the dog. "I have her. Why not wait until after your lunch rush and come check on her. I'll get her settled."

"Are you sure?"

He nodded. "It'll be fine."

Millie grinned. "Thanks, we appreciate it."

Dane turned and walked away. Millie held the door

for Aunt Bea.

Aunt Bea patted her cheek. "Such a nice young man."

"Don't know about young." Millie watched him for a moment. She glanced across the street. A man stood beneath the shadow of a doorway. He frowned at her, then backed up until she couldn't see him. Millie shook her head. "Strange people." She returned to the bakery. Saturday was about to get busy.

12

Even with a full day of rest on Sunday, Millie stretched to relieve tiredness as she got out of the car Monday morning. Stella let go of Luna and the dog bounded across the front seat. "Not so fast," Millie muttered as she grabbed Luna before she could hop from the car. With the leash secured, Luna pushed off from the seat. "I'll run her to the bookstore." Millie tossed keys to Stella.

"What do you want me to start with?"

"I'll be back before you get all the lights on."

"Sure, you will." Stella grinned as she shut the car door. "What do you want me to start just in case?"

Millie stuck out her tongue and turned in the direction Luna pulled on the leash. Within a minute, Stella joined her. "What are you doing?" Millie asked when she noticed her by her side.

"There's a little problem opening the store. Thought I'd walk through Book Shop instead of going all the way around."

"What do you mean?"

"The locks are iced."

Dane opened the door after the first knock. Luna gave her customary greeting, running around his legs while yapping. Millie and Stella stood in the doorway looking at him. "What?"

Stella pulled her glasses down to see over the black rim. "Can't get in the back door."

"Why not?" Dane reached for Luna. The dog kissed his cheek.

"Someone iced the lock."

He held up his hand. "Wasn't me."

Millie shook her head. "Of course not." She glared at Stella. "We can open the front door and go through to the back. The sun will melt the ice in no time."

Dane took the leash. "Let me get Luna situated and come take a look."

Stella ran a finger along a shelf of books. "Never been in here. I thought there would be rows of books and stacks everywhere."

Dane laughed. "That's what your sister thought."

"I like how you have each room set up differently. Makes a cozy feel." Stella commented as they walked along the hallway and considered each of the rooms.

"Over here, there's even a fridge."

Millie remained inside the back door as Stella and Dane walked away, Luna following them with the happy bounce that was her. Breakfast of toast and marmalade turned in her stomach and she suddenly felt ill. *There's no time to be sick.* Millie scolded herself. She shook off the odd feeling and walked the direct route to the front door. "Can I get those keys back from you if you're going to dilly dally?" Millie hollered.

"Almost there," Stella assured. The next moment, she turned the corner with Dane a few steps behind.

Millie opened the door. Stella paused. "Your eyes are looking a bit green this morning."

"My eyes aren't green." Millie frowned.

Stella grinned and kept walking.

"I'm not heating the outside."

"Yes, dad." Millie shot back. She was through the door before he had a chance to respond.

"How does somebody do this?" Stella yelled.

Millie hurried her pace. "No."

"Yes. This lock is iced as well."

"Yoo-hoo, girls." An elderly woman's voice hollered from a little way off. "What seems to be the problem?"

As Millie turned, the elderly woman stumbled and fell to the ground. Both She and Stella cried out. Millie ran. "Aunt Lettie," she gasped.

"Don't try to get up," Stella warned, placing a hand on Aunt Lettie's shoulder.

"What happened?" Dane appeared beside them.

"Oh, my." Aunt Lettie struggled to push Stella's hand away. "Too much fuss. Let me sit up." But as Aunt Lettie tried to move, she gave a gasp of pain.

"I told you to stay still," Stella held her.

Dane took off his jacket. "Here, lay your head on your purse and we'll cover you up."

Millie caught his eye, heart pounding. "We can't get into the bakery to call for an ambulance."

"I'll take care of it." Dane pulled a cell from his back pocket as he tried to tuck his coat around Aunt Lettie.

"It has to be freezing, lying on the ground." Stella held one of her hands.

"Don't know what happened." Aunt Lettie blinked. "I was walking along and lost my footing."

Millie checked the sidewalk but didn't see anything in the way. There wasn't any ice either.

"What were you doing here this morning? You know most of the shops close for Mondays."

"Barbara couldn't do my hair Saturday. She agreed I could come today."

"I'll let her know as soon as you get taken care of." Millie searched the street. "What's taking so long?" It couldn't be healthy for a seventy-year old to lay on the freezing sidewalk.

"I hear them," Dane squeezed her shoulder. "They must be getting close."

Relief washed through her as the ambulance and a cruiser pulled to the curb. The men who stepped out took over the situation. After a few questions, they brought a long orange board.

"We're going to roll you up on your side and then lay you down."

"Can't you just help me up?" Aunt Lettie's voice wobbled with fear.

"It's okay, we're here." Millie reassured her. "I'll call Aunt Bea. She'll find you and stay by your side until you're all fixed up and ready to go home."

Aunt Lettie gave a painful cry as they lifted her side to place the board beneath her. Millie grabbed Dane's hand, holding back tears of concern.

He offered his phone. "Do you know Aunt Bea's number?"

"Of course." Millie pressed the number into his phone and waited for her aunt to pick up.

"Good morning, Mr. Dane. Does this mean my book has arrived?" Aunt Bea's cheerful answer helped center Millie.

"Good morning. It's Millie, actually."

"Millie? What are you doing with Mr. Dane's

phone?"

Millie watched as Aunt Lettie was loaded into the ambulance. "Aunt Lettie fell. They're taking her to the hospital now. Do you think you can meet her there?"

"Of course. What happened? Is she okay?"

"She's in pain."

"I'll call her grandson on the way. He's in town now."

"Thanks, Auntie. She was scared, but I told her you'd meet her at the hospital."

"Good. Best get a move on it. I might be able to beat the ambulance."

Millie didn't doubt Aunt Beatrice could cross town faster than the ambulance. Millie offered the phone to Dane and realized she still knelt on the sidewalk even though the ambulance was leaving.

He pulled her to her feet. "Let's see about that lock."

A layer of ice covered the key opening of the front door. There hadn't been wintery weather, but with temperatures dropping and remaining below freezing thus far into the day, what covered the lock hadn't melted much. Stella rubbed her hands together "I'll run down to Barbara, let her know about Aunt Lettie."

Millie tried to brush the ice away, but it didn't work. "Do you have deicer?"

Dane nodded. "In the trunk of my car."

Millie put her keys in her pocket and walked with Dane toward the bookstore. "Why does everybody call you Dane? I pretty much forgot you had a first name until Aunt Bea was calling you Mr. Dane."

"Your aunt is a proper lady, and with a name like Baxter, is it any wonder?"

"What's wrong with Baxter? It's a distinguished name."

"Try living with it for a while."

"Our mom loved old names." Millie pointed to herself. "Millicent Imogene. Stella's is Estelle, although if you call her that she'll probably deck you."

"You should understand, then. What happened to your mom?" He held the door for her.

"They went to a concert on the other side of the mountain. Weather changed during the evening and they never made it home. Stella and I fell asleep on Aunt Bea's bed. Next morning, she woke us up and said we'd be staying with her from then on."

"That's terrible."

Luna barked as they passed. Millie leaned over the gate to give the dog a hearty rub. With a kiss to the top of her head, Millie straightened and continued after Dane. "My parents were odd. I don't doubt they loved us, but we were young, and they liked to do things we couldn't do. We spent more of our childhood with Aunt Bea than with them. I used to feel guilty because going home felt stranger than staying with Aunt Bea."

They reached his car. In a moment, he had a gallon of antifreeze. "Shall we try the back door?"

"I've got keys," Millie jingled her pocket. "Lead on."

He poured antifreeze over the lock. "Hmm, do you have a towel?"

"I don't hang laundry outside in the winter." His glance made her giggle. "Possibly in the car. Let me look."

She found a towel, and after a few minutes wiping at the lock, the ice dripped away. He poured more antifreeze on the key before inserting it. "Success!" They both cheered.

For a moment, only for a moment, butterflies took flight in Millie's stomach. His grin, the glitter of his eyes. He could have bent and kissed her, and she would have let him. Stella broke the mood.

"Barbara is a dear. She asked us to let her know when we have news. Did you get the door open?"

Dane pushed the door. It swung into the bakery. "All cleaned up, though I would like to know who did this. It wasn't an easy task."

Thought of their prankster turned Millie from thoughts she didn't need to be having. "Why ice the locks? What purpose did it serve?"

Stella dropped her purse on a counter and pulled off her coat. "We heard Aunt Lettie. She might have laid on the sidewalk for a while before a visitor saw her. We wouldn't have heard her in here."

"A blessing in disguise." Millie agreed. "Do you think the front will open okay?" Millie asked as she turned on the lights. Stella headed through to the front.

Dane lifted the mostly full gallon of antifreeze. "If the lock won't move, I can add antifreeze on the outside."

He followed Stella, allowing Millie a chance to collect herself. Kissing was not part of the plan. Stella and Dane must have succeeded, because Stella was alone when Millie walked into the café. "Everything else seem okay?"

"Yes," Stella flipped the open sign on. "Such an odd thing to do."

"If anything else happens, maybe we should let the police know. They can drive through town more frequently during the night."

Stella followed Millie into the kitchen. "Good thing you weren't here at four this morning trying to open those locks."

"I may have agreed to open the bakery Mondays until Christmas, but there's no way I'm getting up that early. Get coffee brewing. I should have muffins in the oven in twenty."

With the bakery closed for Monday, Millie and Stella focused on orders. Millie checked the cakes in the oven. Almost ready. "Three weeks to Christmas. Has Aunt Bea called with an update on Aunt Lettie?"

Stella shook her head. "I tried calling. Oh, wait," Stella pulled the phone from her pocket. "This is her. Aunt Bea?" Stella pressed a button to let Millie hear as well. "What's happened?"

"Oh, girls. I'm glad you were there. She's cracked her hip, but the doctor says they can pin the bone. They won't need to do a hip replacement."

Millie put her hand on Stella's shoulder. "Is she okay?"

"She's in surgery."

"We should come to the hospital." Stella declared.

"Oh, no. Hugh and Allison are here. I know you're working. Allison called Angela to fill in for her. We'll know more this afternoon."

Stella looked at Millie. "We'll stop by the hospital tonight."

"She'll be sleeping."

Millie smiled. "That's okay. We just want to see her. We won't wake her. Promise."

"I'll call when she's out of surgery."

The call ended, and Stella returned her phone to her pocket. "A little slip and she breaks her hip?"

Millie shook her head. "I'm not ready for them to be old yet."

13

Hugh heard the jingle of the bell attached to the door as he pushed into the bakery. The scent of holiday spice washed over him. Familiar rumbles of the café made him regret bringing the other man. Almost. Images of Grandmother in the hospital bed trying to reassure him were not displaced by the colorful Christmas cheer of Bake-n-Cake.

"Hugh!" Stella surged from behind the counter. Her glasses today were thick blue rims shaped like glasses from the fifties. She stopped in front of him. "How is Aunt Lettie? Is Aunt Bea still with her?"

"Mrs. Long was coming in as I left this morning."

"When are you going to get over this Mrs. And Mr. thing and just call her Aunt Bea like the rest of us?"

"Sorry, Stella." He took a deep breath. "I need you to meet my guest."

Stella glanced at the man and shrugged. "Why?"

"This is JT Reynolds, of Reynolds and Beane."

She tilted her head and tapped her red upper lip. "Why is his name familiar?"

The man unbuttoned his gray wool duster. "Because we have offices in every major city between here and Philadelphia."

"A lawyer?" She seemed puzzled.

"Yes." Hugh tried to swallow but his throat was dry. "He... we want to find out why Leticia Keyes fell and broke her hip."

"I know. It's horrible. I can't imagine the pain she must be experiencing."

JT glanced around the room. "There's a good chance the fault may become the responsibility of the bakery."

"The bakery?" Stella backed up a step. "You think we did this to her? But the accident happened out there, not in here."

Hugh crossed his arms. "People report games going on. Weren't the locks frozen yesterday?"

"Your grandmother falling had nothing to do with ice on the locks, I can assure you of that."

JT spoke, "What kind of insurance do you have, Miss Cooke?"

Stella's eyes narrowed, turning darker. "Our insurance isn't involved."

"Mrs. Keyes fell on the sidewalk in front of your store. It was your responsibility to make sure the sidewalk was obstacle free."

Stella got nearer, her voice growing quiet but deadly. "First, I'm going to disagree with your assessment of where the accident occurred. Second, now is not the time for this. I have work to do. You can call and make an appointment and we can sit down to discuss your misconceptions." Her eyes caused a chill to shiver Hugh's back. "Hugh, I wouldn't have thought it of you. I won't say a word to Aunt Bea. She'd tell your grandmother for sure." With that, Stella turned and flounced back to the counter. The thought of her angry with him made him want to take back every word.

"You going to let her talk to you that way?" JT interrupted his thoughts.

"She's right. Now isn't a good time."

"Of course not. Later, she'll have another excuse."

"This is a small town and Mrs. Long is Grandma Keyes' best friend. I'm not about to harm her nieces."

"Negligence on their part is why your grandmother is in the hospital. How many other codes are they out of compliance with?"

Hugh didn't like the feel in his gut. He considered the lawyer. "What's your agenda here?"

"Making sure people like your grandmother don't get caught in the middle. Remember, she's the one who got hurt."

"I am well aware." The reminder irritated him. "I think we're done here."

TJ's glower did not help Hugh's unease.

14

Bright lights gleamed overhead and a sterile sting to the nose meant Millie had no desire to linger. The clank of her shoes matched Stella's as they walked together. They reached Aunt Lettie's hospital room as an unpleasant voice spoke from inside.

"All I need is for you to sign this."

"What are you doing?" Millie asked as she spied a thin lanky man bending over Aunt Lettie who looked ill at ease and more than a little pained.

"Get away from her!" Stella declared, charging to the bed.

"This is a private matter between me and my client."

"I don't think hovering over your client when she's on pain meds is a good time to be doing business." Stella pushed her royal blue glasses firmly into place.

"What business?" Millie didn't care for the man's slicked-back hair and heavy use of cologne.

"This is the lawyer Hugh had with him earlier today."

JT frowned at them both. "You see? This is my business."

"Why isn't Hugh with you now?" Millie swatted him out of the way and took hold of Aunt Lettie's hand.

"How are you?"

"Why is he still here? I told him to go away." Aunt Lettie's hand fisted.

Millie put a hand to her side and glared at the man.

He didn't seem dissuaded. "Hugh wants you to sign the papers."

"Then she'll take care of it when Hugh is with you."

"You don't want her to be taken care of."

"Aunt Lettie is as dear to us as flesh and bone." Stella refused to be intimidated. "We are taking care of her. Leave or I call security."

He bent over a brown duffel bag and shoved the papers inside. With a click, the lid locked, and he stood, holding the case. "You are making things harder on yourselves, wait and see."

Millie made eye contact with Stella as Aunt Lettie shifted on the bed. There wasn't time to be concerned with what he said. She focused on Aunt Lettie instead. "What do you need?"

The anxious look on her weathered face faded away and the grin she gave to the sisters belied the pained stance earlier.

"You little trickster," Millie laughed.

Aunt Lettie squeezed her hand. "They've been generous with pain killers, but I didn't want him to know that. Rude. Men like him give lawyers a bad reputation."

Stella pulled a chair to the bed and sat. "Hugh said you had surgery yesterday."

"Better off than Humpty." She nodded, eyes growing heavy. "They put me back together again."

"Sleep. It'll help you heal all the better. We'll come tomorrow after work and bring your favorite muffin."

Aunt Lettie answered with a quiet snore. Millie kissed her forehead and Stella did the same. They walked out of the hospital. Stella's voice darkened. "I'm going to call Hugh and give him a piece of my mind. How dare he send that man to harass his grandmother."

"Don't jump to conclusions. If Hugh thought it was the right thing, he'd have been here with him. The lawyer came on his own. I wish I knew what he was after."

"Police reports clearly show she was not in front of the bakery. I'm still calling Hugh. If he didn't send the lawyer, he needs to know that jerk showed up anyway."

"I'm going to pick up the dog and head home. Try to get Hugh to meet you. It'll be easier to gauge if he's telling the truth face to face."

"I think I will." Stella narrowed her eyes. The bob of her head made her curls bounce. "If he sent JT, I'm throwing a glass with water at him."

Millie grabbed Stella's arm. "Well, speak of the devil,"

Stella looked across the parking lot and frowned. Hugh had his arms wrapped over his chest, collar up, and his head burrowed as best he could, walking toward the hospital entrance. He liked his fleece-lined suede jacket too well. The man would freeze if he got stuck outside for any length of time. Stella didn't mind his wide shoulders and tussled dirty blond hair. Or his blue-gray eyes. He hadn't been as good looking when they dated back in high school. She stepped in front of him as he hurried to the hospital.

He stopped with a jolt. "Everything alright?"

Stella put her hands on her hips. "As long as you

keep your lawyer friend away from Aunt Lettie."

Hugh glanced from Stella to Millie. "What lawyer friend?"

Stella slapped at his arm. "What's his name? JT? You brought him into the bakery."

"He is not a friend," Hugh shook his head. "I met him right after hearing what happened to Grandmom."

"If he isn't a friend, why bring him?"

"Bring him where?" He shivered. "Can we do this inside? I'm freezing."

"Should buy a more sensible coat. One that's actually meant for winter."

"I'm going." He took a step toward the hospital.

"We have to get back to work. Meet me at the bakery after your visit."

"I won't be available until five."

"Then I'll see you at five. If you're a minute late, I'm feeding your apple cinnamon muffin to our dog." Stella walked away.

"Sweets aren't good for dogs," Hugh called after her.

Millie nudged her sister. "We're mad at him, but you still offer an apple cinnamon muffin?"

Stella grinned. "Surest way to get the truth out of him."

"Uh, huh. Now who's crushing?"

Stella scoffed. "Been down that road. Not going back."

At five minutes before five, Stella placed a plate with a large apple cinnamon muffin on the round table near the front window of the bakery. As expected, a minute later, Hugh walked in. She tapped the table to get his attention. "Always could count on you to be early."

"Next time I'll adjust my watch. Make sure I'm not predictable."

"You can't help yourself. Why bother?"

He sat, still wearing his jacket. He sniffed the muffin. "Is this you or Millie?"

"Millie takes care of most of the baking. I like icing. Did you see the men in the window?"

"You mean the ones wearing boxers with shoulder straps?"

"Those are not boxers, they're lederhosen. Did your degree come with any lessons in culture?"

"My degree is fine."

"Here I thought you were a history major."

"Ha. Why don't you tell me what the lawyer said?"

"You hired him. Shouldn't you know?"

"I did not hire him."

"Then why was he at the hospital?"

"I don't know. I need to hear what happened."

Stella sat across from him. "He was trying to get her to sign papers. I never saw them. He shoved them into his briefcase. He said we can expect trouble."

"This makes no sense. I told him we weren't interested in pursuing anything."

Stella studied Hugh as he ate part of the muffin. The man she'd known wouldn't lie. But how much change came with a decade? "Where did you meet him?"

"At Dunkin Donuts. Like I said, right after hearing from Aunt Bea."

She raised a brow. "Seriously? Dunkin Donuts?"

"It's what I'm used to."

"Can DD make a muffin as good as that?" She pulled a piece of muffin and popped it into her mouth.

Hugh frowned, pulling his plate closer. "Course not."

"Then there's no need to go anywhere else."

"Hopefully, you're cheaper than DD."

"We're better than DD. Quality is worth the price."

"Tell my grandmother and her friends to give me a raise." Hugh's lips twitched.

"We'll slip a subliminal message in their coffee."

He laughed. "Do you remember when we tried that with the fortune cookies? I think we ruined a few dozen trying to find a way to remove the paper without breaking the cookie."

"You were breaking them on purpose to eat them."

He took a drink of coffee. "Enough about the past. I'm sure you have better things to do than reminisce."

"Keep an eye on Aunt Lettie for one thing. Make sure the lawyer doesn't go back. How did you meet him?"

"I went straight from the donut place to the hospital. He was pacing in the waiting area when Aunt Bea told me what happened."

"That's odd. What was he doing there?"

"He commented on something I said, but never mentioned why he was there. He was certain the bakery had to be at fault for Grandmom Keyes' accident."

"Why would he think that? What does he mean pestering Aunt Lettie?"

"I called their offices and told them not to bother her. The secretary promised to give him the message."

"Well done, Hugh."

He finished the last crumb of muffin. "Care to show me around?"

"We close at three which is why the café side is

empty."

"I'm sorry…"

She waved off his attempt to apologize. "We went to the hospital after lunch, so we're late cleaning up. Come on, the kitchen is amazing."

They stood. Hugh grabbed his plate, swiping the few crumbs into his hand. Stella led the way to the kitchen. She pushed through the swinging door and stood, allowing him to see. Marble countertops gleamed. "Wow. This is a full kitchen."

"It used to be a restaurant. We took down the plating tower. Don't need it. Those wire racks were shelves. There are two walk-in freezers and a refrigerator."

He pointed at the large tubs on the bottom shelves beneath the counter. "Are those full of cookies?"

"They were cooked today. We'll ice them in the morning to set them in the front window."

"This is amazing. You would love the kitchen at St. Ives. At least, Millie would. Do you like to cook?"

"I don't mind getting to work in this beautiful place."

"When's your day off? I can give you a tour of the mansion and carriage house."

"Seriously? I would love that. I've been dying to see inside since they finished the renovations."

He chuckled. "There are more projects in the works. I doubt the house will ever be finished. You can come see, though."

"How about Sunday? I'm meeting Millie for dinner, but I'm free all afternoon."

"Sunday, it is. Want to meet me there or should I pick you up?"

"No need to drive to town. I'll meet you at noon. I'll bring a picnic basket."

"Muffins and chicken salad?"

She put her hands on her hips. "You do not remember my chicken salad."

He held up his hand. "I have never liked anyone else's."

She rolled her eyes. "Such a ham."

"I'll see you Sunday?"

"Yes."

His smile gave her a tingle.

15

"Ms. Cooke?" Allison stuck her head through the kitchen door. "Um, there's a man in the café to see you."

Millie looked around. "Ms. Cooke?"

Allison shuffled. "Well, he says he's an inspector."

"Between Thanksgiving and Christmas?" Millie wiped her hands on her apron as she crossed the kitchen. "Where is he?"

Allison pointed. "He took a seat at the table against the wall."

Millie recognized the slightly balding jovial man. She walked across the room. "Bill, how are you?" She held her hand toward him as she reached the table.

He stood. "Hello, Millie."

"Can I get you something?"

"Afraid I'm here on business. I'm not able to get any of your scones."

"You were here, what, five months ago? A bit early for another inspection?"

"Let's call this one a surprise. Can you get me your health inspection letter?"

"Of course. The one on the wall behind the register or the one filed in the office?"

"I'll take the one from the office."

It didn't take long for Millie to return with the document. Bill tapped an empty space in the middle. "A claim was filed that your facility is not properly maintained."

"Facility? Do you mean the building? We lease from an owner in Minneapolis."

"Maintenance is still your responsibility. How often do you take care of the filters?"

"Every three months. Stella makes sure they are cleaned properly."

"What about the fryer?"

"We take care of that weekly and the outside venting is checked at the same time as the other filters."

"What do you use to deice the front and back?"

"Mainstreet maintenance is responsible for that. It's a salt/sand mixture. I sweep once everything dries up. Do you think this has to do with Aunt Lettie falling?"

Bill shrugged. "I thought it might, but I checked the records and she wasn't in the vicinity of the bakery."

"Why does it seem like someone wants people to think she was?"

He laughed. "You're asking me to explain what people are thinking? Half the time I'm not sure they do."

Millie shook her head. "You're terrible. Your poor wife must be crazed."

"She will be when I call and tell her she has to come to town for a bag of scones."

"Can I return to baking? You know you're welcome to look at anything."

"You run a tight ship, Millie. If I find anything while I'm poking around, I'll show you what you need to do."

"I appreciate your support, Bill. Thanks to you, I know how to get to the filters on the fridge." Millie returned to the kitchen.

Stella caught up with her a few moments later. "Allison said an inspector was here."

Millie nodded. "It's Bill. He says a concern was filed. He's always been fair with us. I don't think we have to worry about him."

"But why write a complaint? Why not come to us?" Stella tapped her foot then pointed to the front. "Why does Aunt Lettie's fall come to mind? I bet that nasty lawyer in involved."

"Why? What does he have against our bakery?"

"You don't think your book buddy—"

Millie interrupted Stella. "No, he would not."

Stella held up her hand. "Maybe he made a complaint before you started getting along."

"Dane would never intentionally cause harm, any more than I would."

Stella smiled. "I know. I wanted to see how hard you would protest." She started to walk away.

Millie frowned at her back. "What do you mean? What's that supposed to mean?" Millie yelled after her, but Stella ignored her.

"What's wrong?" Bill stepped into the kitchen.

"Nothing unusual. Just my sister being a brat."

He laughed. "I have a few myself."

Millie wiped flour from her hands on her apron. "Have you found any problems?"

"None." Bill handed her the inspection report with another seal of approval.

Millie sighed. "Good to hear. Thank you."

"My wife will be in later. No special treatment. Don't want anyone to claim I can be bribed."

Millie chuckled. "Goodbye, Bill. Have good holidays. Next time, try not to startle my staff."

He headed out with a wave. "Always fun when there's a newbie."

16

Midmorning Sunday, Stella drove south
of town to the fork leading past the river. The St. Ives
mansion and carriage house were idyllically situated on
a knoll overlooking the river. Edgar Ives had been one
of the original investors with Ford Motor Company.
The eccentric bachelor had a penchant for European
castles and built his mansion with turrets and rounded
wings. Instead of narrow arrow holes, the mansion
boasted long, wide windows with sweeping views of
hills, the river, and woods in the distance. But it was not
a massive castle.

"Only about ten thousand square feet, not counting
attics and basement," Hugh explained as he held the car
door.

"Yeah, not massive at all." Stella laughed. "It looks
immense from a distance."

"We can walk around this way and come in through
the kitchen." He led Stella around a cobbled path. The
stone exterior had a few creeping ivies.

Stella touched one of the dead leaves. "I'm
surprised they handle winter."

Hugh slapped his hand on a rock. "Fireplace must
warm it enough to make do."

"Is that the carriage house?" Stella spied a long building with three sets of wooden arched doors.

"Yes. It has three bays on either side. This side will be the gift shop, and the other side used for storage." He pulled on an iron loop to open the rounded top wood door.

"It's modern." Stella was surprised to see stainless steel, wide plank wood floors, and traditional cabinets that went to the tin ceiling. "This is beautiful." She rubbed her fingers across the cream-colored counters.

"These counters and backsplash keep the kitchen from looking like a cave."

"They're planning to have functions here."

"Perfect location for parties and weddings. Wait till you see the staircase in the grand foyer."

"Can you imagine coming here for Christmas or New Year's Eve?"

"Would be perfect. Come through here." He led her into a large dining room. "This is actually five tables put together." The long table covered with a red tablecloth had twenty place settings decorated for Christmas.

The formal dining room had the same cream-color on the lower two thirds of the walls. A high plate rail separated the deep blue above. On the far side from the kitchen was a fireplace. "That would be large enough for Santa." Stella bent to try to see up the chimney.

"Don't disturb the bats," Hugh warned with a jab to her ribs.

She glared at him over the top rim of her glasses.

"How do you do that? You've got the librarian marm down pat."

She slapped his arm. "Are you planning to hang

paintings on the walls?"

"A few from the Ives collection will be showcased on this level. The museum feel will be more upstairs. There are fourteen bedrooms and a long gallery."

"You have to fill fourteen rooms?"

"The east wing are family bedrooms. We'll set them as they would have been in early twentieth century."

"I thought Ives was a confirmed bachelor?"

"Wait until you see these." He took her hand and led her to an office. The three desks were piled with books, objects, and papers. More boxes were stacked on the floor.

"I see you're as organized as ever." She frowned at the mess.

He ignored her. "We found letters." He handed her a plastic-encased yellowing sheet of paper. The handwriting was firm and legible.

"My dear Edgar," Stella read. "Seeing you at R's this weekend brought back many memories. I regret my hasty words to you, and desperately wish to accept your proposal. I am a foolish woman not to have realized my love for you." Stella looked up. "Who is R? Rockefellers? Is Mildred a Rockefeller? Did they marry?"

"I have found three letters so far. They are engaged in the last two."

"Let me see." Stella grabbed them, absently setting her black-rimmed glasses on her head. "She's coming to plan his Christmas party and the wedding is to be at Easter. What is she thinking? It will still be too cold."

Hugh tapped the letters in Stella's hand. "What happened between Christmas and Easter to stop the wedding? There has never been any indication that

Edgar married."

"Why couldn't they make history this interesting when we were in school?"

"Unanswered questions—"

"Drive me crazy." She finished for him. "You'll let me know when you find out anything else?"

"Of course."

They walked the rest of the first floor. "This would be a perfect place to host a Christmas party. Have a tree stand in front of each of those windows."

"Great minds think alike. We hid plugs in the floor in front of each window."

"When will the mansion be ready to open?"

"It's practically ready now. They ordered merchandise for the gift store. Grandmom will help set it to order."

"Not you, huh?" Stella teased. "Will she use antique displays?"

He nodded "There's plenty of old furniture still here."

"Any plans to restore the gardens?"

"A few years down the road."

"You all are doing amazing work. Don't forget about Bake-n-Cake if you need catered sweets."

"Don't worry, not a chance I'm forgetting the bakery. Ready to head upstairs?"

Although there were no windows in the hallway, most of the bedroom doors were open and light streamed through. "I didn't realize they had indoor plumbing in the early nineteen hundreds." Stella peeked at a bathroom with a large porcelain clawfoot tub.

"Imagine tiling this."

Yellow tiles started at the floor, went up the walls,

and across the ceiling. "I can't keep the tiles in my bathroom clean and these things are over a hundred years old? What's the secret?"

"I have a feeling it's quality. These are the family rooms. We have a bedroom and a sitting room for Edgar. His mother's room has a beautiful desk."

"Did you find a hidden compartment?"

"Never looked." They crossed the hall to a small bedroom. The walls were papered pale green with tiny white flowers.

"This must be original." Stella admired, brushing her fingers across the glossy surface of the desk.

Hugh tapped one of the walls. "The closet door blends. See if you can find it."

She moved to the wall nearest to her and tapped, but it thudded like a solid wall. She skipped the outside wall with the two windows. On the other side, she tapped, and the thud was lighter. "Here it is." She looked up. "Maybe." Yes, there was the line to show where the door moved. "How do you open it?"

He pushed, and the door clicked and sprang into the room.

"How clever. That needs to be part of the tour. Or a special behind the scenes tour like they do at Biltmore. Do you think he knew the Vanderbilt's?"

"He must have. I think they all traveled in the same circles."

"What's next?"

He led her down the hall. "This will be one of the first exhibit rooms."

The room he led her to was large with white walls and built ins beneath the windows. She sat on a cabinet. "What was this used for?"

"Would have been a nursery. It's been empty all this time. The plan is to put a few model cars up here."

"How would you get cars upstairs?"

"They'll come in pieces and we'll assemble them in the room. Ives money came from the auto industry, thought it would be fitting to honor that in this space."

"It does seem large enough. Put a few mannequins with period-appropriate dress near the cars."

"Why would we do that?"

"If anyone isn't interested in the cars, they might come in to see the clothes."

Hugh rubbed his chin, nodding. "Good point. Hope you don't mind that I use it."

The museum rooms were empty, although wrapped frames in a variety of sizes leaned against the wall. Hugh brought Stella to the main staircase in the front of the house. "How do you like this?"

The banister was a deep mahogany wood with wrought iron balusters that curved to the ground floor. The chandelier that hung in the space had the same mixture of wood and metal. "I imagine any woman looks like a princess gliding down these stairs." Stella made her way down the stairs, being sure to hold her arms out and hands up. She sighed upon reaching the bottom and turned to watch Hugh. "You'll have to convince the society to hold a Christmas party here next year."

"The Widow Peeps would appreciate that." Hugh rubbed his hand on the banister. "One of these days I'm going to slide down."

"You are not. Or you better not by yourself. You'll fall and get hurt."

"Thanks for the vote of confidence, brat." He

laughed. "How about we get the picnic basket and head to the gazebo?"

"In the summer. Today, I say we eat in that beautiful kitchen. I promise to wash up anything we mess."

"Fine," he grunted.

17

A few days later, Stella flipped the switch to light up the display cases. The jingle of the bell over the door caused her to turn around.

"Aunt Bea, how are you this morning? Up early, aren't you?" Stella reached across the front counter to give a hug.

"Good morning, dear. I'm up early because Dahlia must shop in Minneapolis today. She insists it will be the least crowded day between now and Christmas."

Stella laughed. "That's not saying much."

"Ergo, I require caramel coffee and a butter crumb muffin." She leaned closer and lowered her voice. "Lots of crumb. I intend Dahlia to have to spend tomorrow cleaning out the car."

"Understood. You want the drink to go?"

"Don't worry, I shan't spill a drink. That would be mean."

Stella prepared Aunt Bea's order as Aunt Dahlia and Grandma Cooke walked into the café. "Too bad Aunt Lettie's laid up with her broken hip. You'd be the four amigos."

"Three musketeers will suffice. Although," Dahlia waved her phone, "Leticia insisted on my being able to sky with her while we're shopping."

"You mean skype?"

"That's what I said." Dahlia nodded and winked.

"Do you want coffee as well?"

"I'll take mine black with cream."

Stella swallowed her grin. There was no point trying to explain the issue with her order. Dahlia like things her way.

"There you are," Stella set a cup carrier with a stack of napkins between two drinks. "Drive safe. I don't want to visit anyone else in the hospital."

"Anything special you and your sister are hoping for Christmas?"

"Blue skies and good business."

"If only everyone were like you. I could save on gas." Dahlia lifted the cup tray. "Have a good day, girls."

"Same to you. Don't talk to any strange men."

She wiggled her eyebrows. "How will I know they're strange until I talk to them?"

Stella shook her head.

The café quieted once the three older women left. It was a few minutes after seven. Stella nabbed her mp3 player and hooked into the sound system. A few swipes later, the melody of Silent Night spread through the room. Cleaning windows came next. The shelves were ready for the day's special. She pushed into the kitchen. "Wow. That smells like cinnamon buns." Sure enough, Millie had trays of golden sweetbread swirled with brown sugar and topped with butter cream icing. "Did you save me one of these?"

Millie pointed at a covered plate on the back counter. "For lunch."

Stella picked up a tray. "Hope I can wait that long."

"Did I hear Aunt Bea?" Millie continued icing the treats.

"Three of them are heading into Minneapolis for shopping."

Millie sighed. "I still need to get to shopping."

"What about tomorrow?"

"With how busy we are?"

"We can get Angela and Allison to work extra shifts. You take tomorrow afternoon and I'll take Thursday afternoon."

Millie handed her a tray of cinnamon buns. "Bixby is open late Wednesday. That works for me."

"I'll check with Allison when she comes in today and give Angela a call." She backed through the door and turned, finding herself facing a short, round woman. Thankfully, her fingers tightened on the tray instead of dropping it. "Good morning. Didn't see you there."

"No one was in the café. I thought I'd check through the door."

Stella moved the tray. "Today's special. Delectable cinnamon buns. Would you like one?"

"No thank you. I'm here for the owner."

"Oh, hold on. Let me set these down." She pushed the tray onto an empty shelf. She faced their visitor, holding out her hand. "I'm Estelle Cooke, one of the owners."

"Jennifer Grayer." She shook hands and then handed her a business card.

Stella read it. "An inspector?" She gave Jennifer a puzzled look. "We just had one last week."

"Last week? That's odd. Are you having problems

that would concern your customers?"

"Not in here. An elderly woman fell outside on the sidewalk. Further from our shop, not on our property."

"Well. Why don't you let me have a look around?" Jennifer started with the coffee machines, taking them apart and looking at the pieces. "Where did you go to school?" She asked as Stella rearranged the muffin trays.

"I have a degree from Minn State, in business management and accounting."

Jennifer connected the machine parts where they belonged. "My degree was in elementary education. I wanted to stay in Falls Point but there weren't any teaching jobs at the time."

"Seems to be a shortage now."

"Good thing I've kept my teaching certificate current through the years. I plan to take a teaching position in the fall."

"Congratulations. That will be a change for you."

Jennifer grinned. "I don't know. Instead of inspecting soda sprayers, I'll be inspecting homework and center work. Nicely done." She returned the last soda dispense nozzle to the machine. "Most issues come from things like this."

"We try to keep up with cleaning. Let me know if you have any suggestions."

"Stells, when are you getting this other pan of muffins?" Millie called through the doorway.

"Are you ready to see the kitchen?"

"Certainly. Although, by the smell of things, I'll be the one in trouble."

Stella led her through the swinging door. "Just keep your finger out of the icing."

"Who's this?" Millie wiped her hands on her apron.

Jennifer held out a hand. "I'm Jennifer, city inspector. The filed claim said you were having trouble, and here I am."

"Oh. Is that the same claim as the previous inspector, or a new one?" Millie glanced at Stella. Stella shrugged. "Shall I show you around?"

She shook her head. "You look busy."

"Christmas and summer vacations are our busiest seasons."

Stella heard the door ring. "I'm heading to the café." She grabbed the muffins.

The steady revolution of customers marked the typical Tuesday morning. That was until Hugh showed up. Stella didn't realize her shoulders had tensed with the inspection until she felt herself relax. Hold up. Hugh was fun and sweet, but that was it.

"Those look amazing." He pointed at the half full tray of cinnamon buns.

"I've got mine waiting in the back until lunch."

"Why not make it two of them and I'll join you?"

Stella looked at her watch. "Are you waiting four hours?"

"I'm a patient man."

"You are not. The first senior year newspaper was ruined because you didn't want to take time for a decent edit and revision."

He covered his eyes and dropped his head in shame. "Am I never to be forgiven for that mistake?"

She grinned. "Probably not as long as I remember all the details."

"Great. I'll see you at noon. Be sure to save me one of those buns or I'm stealing yours."

"Pest."

"Brat."

He left, but Stella still had a bit more bounce in her step. Not a good sign. But not a bad one either, she decided.

A few more customers passed through, and then Jennifer was standing in front of the register.

Stella did a double take. "Everything okay?"

"Perfect. I explained to your sister. Of course, my stomach would protest if I left without trying one of something, if not everything."

"It's good when the inspector is willing to eat in the establishment, right?"

Jennifer laughed. "Most people wouldn't come right out and say it, but, yes. What do you recommend?"

"Cinnamon buns. Fresh and gooey, I can't wait to have mine."

"Okay, cinnamon bun it is. Add a cup of tea. Best make sure you put one back for that young man. He seemed adamant."

Stella grinned. "He should have gotten one while they're gettable."

Hugh's stomach grumbled as he entered the bakery shortly before one. The main bakery crowd was through. The girl behind the counter wasn't Stella. Where'd she go?

"May I help you?" Angela, he read her name tag, asked.

"I'm here for Stella. We have a meeting that involves cinnamon buns."

"Ah, now I get it. There was a bidding war and she still refused to sell the last one."

His stomach growled. He laughed. "Obviously, I'm

looking forward to it."

"I've got him, Angela." Stella moved through the swinging door carrying two plates, each with a large cinnamon bun. "What would you like to drink?"

"I better go with water."

"Alright. Can you bring us two ice waters, Angela?" Stella led him to a table by a tree painted on the window.

Hugh looked at the mural. "Your artist did a nice job."

"Did you hear what Dane did to it?" They sat.

"What do you mean?"

"Dane and my sister have a competition going on. Well, hopefully over now. I think the goal was to see who could annoy the other the most." She told him about the pranks.

Hugh laughed. "Is it a love hate relationship?"

"I don't know, and I don't ask. Dane was helpful when Aunt Lettie broke her hip. How is she, by the way?"

He leaned closer and lowered his voice. "Have you ever watched old people try to figure out how to use technology? I was at the rehab center trying to help for a little while, but those gals made me seasick. They're trying to show Grandmom a sweater and all we see is Aunt Bea. Then they were turning the phone around and peaking to see if what they wanted to show was on the screen. All we saw were these white and lavender-haired heads getting in the way. I haven't laughed that hard in ages."

"At least that means they made it to Minneapolis safely. I'm not sure the three of them should be driving together. They can barely sit at a table and eat without distracting each other."

"I didn't realize how much they could change in ten years."

"You've changed as well."

"Me?"

"Yes. You're no longer scrawny. You've filled out those wide boney shoulders of yours."

"Hey," Hugh took another bite of the cinnamon bun. "Are you saying I've put on weight since high school."

"In a good way."

"You haven't changed much. You still like your fashionable glasses. And you're shorter than me."

"I'm also still a year younger than you."

"How many times did you tell me you would catch up?"

"Ha. Finish your bun. I've got work to go do." Her own plate was empty.

"Then go work. When will I see you next?"

"I don't know. You've got a big job to do at the Ives Mansion. Focus on that, not me."

"Yes, ma'am." Hugh saluted, but he had no intention of keeping his word.

18

Even though the gray sky promised snow and other wintery mixes, Millie hummed as she scooped the baked gingerbread men onto a wire cooling rack. A dozen trays of Christmas cookies at various stages of complete were for the High School's winter production tomorrow night. She'd played a part back in high school. What was it? Oh yes, an elf.

"How's Mrs. Keyes doing?"

Millie jumped at the sound of Dane's voice invading her kitchen. She turned to the door leading to the café. Sure enough, Dane leaned through. She blinked, but he was still there. "What?"

"Mrs. Keyes? The woman who fell on the sidewalk?"

"You mean Aunt Lettie?"

"Fine." He shook his head. "How is she?"

Millie wiped her hands nervously on her apron. "She's in good spirits. They did surgery to repair the break. Should be able to go home in a few days."

"That's great news."

Millie smiled. "I plan to stop in after work today and then go shopping in town. Maybe traffic won't be bad mid-week."

"Want company?"

"What?" She couldn't have heard him correctly.

"It's okay." He shrugged. "You probably don't want a virtual stranger tagging along. Forget I asked." He made to turn and leave.

"I don't mind," Millie blurted, then fought the urge to cover her mouth. What was she doing?

His grin was hopeful. "Are you sure?"

It was Millie's turn to shrug, and then she nodded. "Aunt Lettie wants to thank you for your help."

"Glad I was there."

"Same here. Um, would three o'clock be too early for you?"

"Nah, I can bring the dog to your house. Put her in the bathroom, or will Stella be home? Is Stella shopping, too?"

"No, Stella will be home after work. I want to get a gift for her."

"Okay. Good." His chest moved with a deep breath. "I can drive, if you like."

***

Dane shoved his hands in his pockets. What was he doing? He hadn't intended to come into the bakery for an expensive designer hot chocolate. He hadn't intended to visit the kitchen to say hello to Millie. He certainly never intended to spend several hours in her company. Christmas shopping? What was he thinking?

He needed presents for his sister and niece. Mom and Dad too, although the department store frenzy wasn't likely to help with them. He cleared his throat. "I should get back to work."

"Same. Got to finish these orders before I can leave. Stella had to design gingerbread men in lederhosen.

Now everybody wants a dozen."

"Is that what I smell?" He stepped further into the kitchen instead of out of it. "That was my absolute favorite. I used to sit on a stool in my grandmother's kitchen and watch her make them."

Millie sighed and held out one of the iced cookies.

"Are you sure?" He asked even though he was already reaching for it.

"I always bake enough for broken pieces. Rather have a few extras than not enough."

He took it before she could rescind the offer. He bit an arm. The satisfying crunch led to the sweet burst of molasses paired with vanilla cream icing. It was perfect. He groaned. "I hope you teach Becky how to make these. It's delicious."

"Go back to work. You aren't getting anymore." Though she dismissed him and went back to designing what was laid out on the counter, the red in her cheeks proved she appreciated his comment. He was nearly to the swinging door when he heard her clear her throat.

"You can call the bakery if something comes up and the visit to Aunt Lettie won't work today."

He turned with one hand on the door. She was bent over the counter but peeked at him. He wasn't backing out. "I'll see you at three."

Knowing he looked forward to an outing made him want to whistle as he traversed the cold from the bakery to Book Shop. Lights were on, book tree safely in place. He went through the front door and managed to calm a couple of children wrestling over a bean bag chair. With a glance from him, they stopped. Their harried mother picked another book and added it to the growing pile in her arms. Dane stepped up to her. "Let me help you with this." He took the stack of books. "I can place them by the front register," he offered as he pointed at the other front room.

"Thank you. We'll be out of your hair in no time."

"Don't worry about it. This room is intended to be enjoyed by children." He walked to the register, depositing the books on the counter.

Luna's tail beat the wood floor as he passed her coup. He leaned over the fence. "How are you doing, girl?" He scratched between her ears. She sat, tilting her head to receive a better rub. "You're a character. Hope you don't mind my going on a shopping spree with your mistress tonight."

"What are you doing?" Traci, the college-age girl he hired for the season, returned discarded books to their shelves.

"I wanted to check on Mrs. Keyes to see how her recovery is. Can you stay and close shop?"

"Sure. I'm saving for a car. Any extra work hours are fine by me as long as they don't interfere with class."

Dane laughed. "Agreed. Keep that stack of books by the register. Tell her she gets a ten percent discount for buying five or more books."

"You intend to make money, right?" She narrowed her black-lined eyes at him.

"Yes. When are finals? I want you to have the study time you need."

"Next week is dead week. I'll study between shifts."

"Good. Watch the front, I've got a few boxes to unpack."

"Sure thing, Mr. Dane."

Dane walked to his office space. Two large boxes

with a small box on top were stacked beside his desk. He placed the small box on his desk, refusing to give in to the excitement of discovering what rare find had come. He used the blade of a pair of scissors to tear through the tape of the first large box. Piles of books filled the space, sending the scent of new paper and ink around him as he bent to remove the books.

The book business wasn't predictable, but hopefully, these new titles would be popular. He stacked them on a book cart finagled from the library. Once the two large boxes were empty, he cut the other end and flattened them. A short walk through the back door took him to the recycle bin.

He caught sight of Millie's car. Looping the ribbon had been a chore, but now he found himself wanting to laugh about it. He returned to the bookstore before the chill settled in his bones. The large leather chair squeaked as he sat at the desk. He pulled the small package closer. With this package, he was much more careful opening. Cornstarch peanuts floated in the air and landed across the desk. Ah, vintage first run of The Hobbit. The green cover was in great shape. He opened to a page toward the middle. It had crisp clear letters and white paper. He would love to have it, but he'd promised himself long ago, didn't matter how rare or how bad he wanted a rare find, every title would have at least two weeks on the shelf as saleable inventory. He rubbed his finger across the cover of the book. Fifteen days and he'd be able to add it to his private collection.

A knock on the door frame caused him to look up at Traci. "Yes?"

She held up a cup with the outline of evergreen trees. "Did you forget why you went to the bakery?"

His hot chocolate. "Oh yeah." He walked over to get his drink. "Must have been thinking about inventory."

"Sure." She grinned. "I hear those sisters at the bakery are pretty cute."

"I hear you want a car and need to keep this job."

"Back to work." She pushed off and returned to the bookstore.

Dane shook his head. "They've been there four years. No reason anything should be different today than it was a year ago." But he drank the hot chocolate anyway.

***

"It's not a date." Millie announced as Stella entered the kitchen.

Stella backed up a step. "What's not a date?"

"I said I was visiting Aunt Lettie and he asked to tag along."

"He?" Stella removed her glasses as she approached her sister. "Dane, he? The man who left without the drink he purchased?"

"Oh, did he?" Millie looked down at the cookie dough she rolled across a plastic mat. "Did you get it to him?"

"Angela took it." Stella leaned against the end of the island. "What's not a date?"

"Nothing." Millie pressed too hard on the dough with the rolling pin. The sugar cookie dough split. She pulled it up to start over. Stella waited silently. Why had she opened her big mouth? "We're going to visit Aunt Lettie and then shop. I was already planning to go to Bixby. That's why Ashley and Angela are here today."

"What are you going to wear to this non-date?"

"What do you mean?" Millie studied her pants and sensible black shoes.

"You can't go like that. Besides, you smell like a cookie and you'd drive any man to distraction. When are you meeting him?"

"He's bringing Luna to the house at three."

Stella grinned. "And you'll take one vehicle because it's silly to take two and follow each other to the same places."

"Of course." What was wrong with that?

"But it's not a date."

"Course not. I don't even like the man."

"Oh, you like him. You might even be a step beyond like."

Millie flicked flour in Stella's direction. "Dane likes women like Nora. I will never be like Nora."

Stella backed away, brushing white from her black sweater. "Nora's not the one going shopping with him," Stella sang as she ran from the kitchen.

Millie huffed, and checked the clock. Still a few hours of work before she'd need to go home and shower. Would he find her irresistible if she didn't wash away the cookie smell? "Don't even go there," she muttered as she pressed cookie cutters into the evenly rolled dough.

Time passed too quickly, and Millie stood freshly showered in front of her closet. "I am not wearing a skirt," she assured herself. She pulled a pair of black work pants. "This works. Tuck in a red blouse." Ordinary. He'd seen her in work clothes before. She hung it back in the closet. What was she doing? She pulled out a long flowery shirt instead. Monet-inspired blooms covered the shirt. She grabbed green leggings to wear with it.

With her hair down, she looked different. Millie frowned at her image in the mirror. She looked like a woman going on a date. But the doorbell rang before she could contemplate a different outfit. She nabbed a hair band as her heart fluttered.

Luna raced in as she opened the front door. Not prepared to face Dane quite yet, she crouched beside the dog. "How are you doing, Luna-loo?" Luna jumped excitedly.

"Let me unleash her before you end up in a tangle." Dane laughed, attempting to get to the hook.

"Too late." Millie slipped onto her backside as Luna danced around her.

"Sit," Dane ordered, and Luna obeyed. "Good girl."

Millie laughed. "Are you talking to me or the dog?"

He offered his hand, and she accepted, allowing him to pull her to her feet. "The dog. I figure I'll have to wait and see about you."

Millie straightened her shirt. "Let me get Luna in the bathroom. Stella's not home yet."

"She doesn't mind you taking off like this?"

"Her turn's tomorrow. Today's the only day Bixby stays open later."

"Bixby?"

"Yes. It's an antique and craft center over in Mayweather."

"Never heard of it."

Millie turned around to face him. "We don't have to go."

"Oh, no. That's great. I thought you'd want to head for the mall."

She made a face. "This close to Christmas? I'd rather visit the dentist."

His smile relaxed. "Agreed."

***

Dane closed the door but remained close as Millie took off after Luna. The sisters' home was cozy with stuffed chairs and light colors. Frames on the walls held more photos of people than artwork. He could see an office with a cluttered desk. Seemed familiar.

Millie reappeared. "Ready. I think Luna's had her share of being cooped up today. She'll be happy when Stella gets here."

He waited until she had her coat on before opening the door. "Which hospital entrance do you use?"

"The back. It's closer to an elevator. Here, let me punch my number in." She said as he pulled the door shut.

"How do you like the electronic deadbolt?"

"I never have to worry about my keys. Very handy."

"You should probably make your code more complex than one, two, three, four."

"Hey, how did you know that?"

"I watched."

She frowned. "You're not supposed to watch."

He opened the car door for her. "I know you can be more clever than that."

She waited for him to come around to the driver side. "I'm creative, not necessarily clever."

"I could not understand why people kept asking me for keys. Half a dozen wanted to know what the secret about the Christmas keys was. It wasn't until your Aunt Lettie told me about the sign that I finally figured it out."

"The Widow Peeps gave us away." Millie sighed. "I still don't think it was quite worth the effort of painting the whole front window of the shop. And then to be cool about it." She slid a glance in his direction. "I bet you're good at poker."

"I have my tells, but no point giving them away this early in the game."

They drove in silence for a bit, allowing the Christmas music to fill the comfortable space between them. Dane started to hum. They reached the hospital. He drove past the emergency entrance, taking the next and following the road around to the back entrance. He shut the door and gave the red brick building a dark look. "Never did like these places." He shook the unsettling urge to skip the visit and went around to open the door for Millie. "We have arrived."

She stepped out, adjusting her colorful shirt. "Better to be guests than patients."

He didn't reply, rather shoved his hands in his pocket and convinced himself to follow Millie through the automatic doors.

Mrs. Keyes seemed like a pale ghost swallowed up by a hospital bed. Dane almost pulled back, but Mrs. Keyes' eyes sparked as she saw the two of them. Millie rushed forward to grasp her hands. He followed.

"Hello, my dear," Mrs. Keyes greeted Millie. Her strong voice belied the diminutive image on the bed.

"How are you today, Aunt Lettie? That lawyer hasn't been back to pester you, has he?"

"I almost hope he does come." She tapped the cane standing beside the bed. "A good wallop is what he needs."

"What lawyer?" Dane moved closer.

Millie waved off his question. "I'll tell you about it in the car."

"Mr. Dane, what a pleasure to see you." Mrs. Keyes stretched her arm toward him.

He wrapped her hand with his. "I've been wanting to see how you are. Millie allowed me to come with her today."

"Thank you for your help, young man."

"Glad I could be there for you. How soon will you get out of here?"

"They'll be moving me to Hill's Rehab when a room opens up."

"I think that's a good plan," Millie said. "They can make sure you get around safely before you're home on your own."

"Like your grandmother would leave me on my own. She'd sleep on a cot here if they let her."

"You have a strong circle of friends. We'll all be around to keep you safe."

Circle of friends? Dane considered the idea as he and Millie walked the long sterile hallway toward the elevator.

"Poor Aunt Lettie. She's not used to relying on others."

"We all have to at one time or another."

"Who do you rely on? Nora?"

"Nora?" Who was… oh, right. He laughed. "Definitely do not rely on Nora."

"She seemed to think differently at the lighting parade."

"She struggles to take no for an answer." Dane pushed the down arrow for the elevator. He grinned.

"Are you trying to find out if I've got something going on with her?"

Millie scoffed, "What? Of course not."

They entered the elevator. "It's okay. My longest relationship was with a border collie named Jazz. Her owner and I were together for a while, but she took off and left Jazz with me."

Millie's arms crossed. "I don't find it hard to believe you do better with a dog than with a human."

They reached the lobby. Dane wished he could take back what he'd said. He wanted to be truthful with Millie, which was surprising and dangerous. He shook off the uncomfortable thoughts. "What about you? Do you have a boyfriend?"

"Not likely. Starting and running the bakery doesn't leave time to socialize."

"Yet here you are with me."

"It's Christmas, and we're shopping. This isn't a date."

They reached the car and he followed her around to the passenger side to open the door. If she had any thought against the gesture, she showed no sign of it. She slipped around him and climbed in. He tightened his hold on the door because he suddenly wanted to take hold of her. Not a good idea. "In?" He asked instead, and then closed the door after she nodded. He breathed and counted to ten as he walked around to the driver's side.

***

Millie felt her chest flutter as she watched Dane climb in. "Mayweather isn't far from here." She showed him the address for Bixby on her smartphone. He entered it into the car's navigation system.

He pushed buttons as he replied, "Mrs. Keyes seems in good spirit."

"She won't let them keep her in rehab for long."

"You know her well, huh?"

"Grew up with her, Grandma Cooke, and Aunt Bea."

"How did you end up with your Aunt and not your grandmother?"

"Aunt Bea is mom's aunt. Grandma Cooke is our grandmother. She moved back to St. Ives after our parents died. We were already settled with Aunt Bea, and there we stayed."

The car's navigation system spoke, and Dane made a left turn. "What's this about a lawyer?"

"Ugh, he's a friend of Hugh's. We saw him harassing Aunt Lettie and made him leave."

"Who's Hugh?"

"Aunt Lettie's grandson. Hugh brought this lawyer to the bakery a few days ago. He thinks the accident was our fault."

"She wasn't anywhere near the bakery. I was there."

"That's what I told Hugh. He has to know if it was our problem, we'd do everything we could to make it right."

"Maybe his interest isn't with his grandmother."

"No way. He adores her. I've known Hugh since he had training wheels on his bike. Stella talked with him last Sunday."

"Instead of you?"

She grinned. "Are you trying to find out about me and Hugh?"

"Course not." He looked around the street. "I thought this place was supposed to be down here."

"It is." Millie pointed. "All the way at the end. Are your parents still around?" Time for a safer topic.

He didn't seem to mind. "Yes. Parents, sister, niece. Dad's a professor at Temple University, in Philly. Mom works at the botanical garden. Sylvia and Becky are a few towns from here. I get to see my niece a lot more than my parents." He parked in the first spot he could find. "Interesting," he commented as he leaned to see through the windshield.

"It's an eclectic shopping center. There are stalls as well as shops and kiosks."

"Reminds me of Reading Market in Philly."

"We don't have to stay long. Let me know when you're ready to go."

He gave her a look. "I asked to come along. You take as much time as you need."

Millie considered her mental list. Grandma Cooke, Aunt Bea, and Stella were the main ones. Finding gifts for Aunt Lettie and maybe Hugh and Angela would be nice as well. She looked at Dane. No, not getting him anything. "Do you have a list?"

He nodded. "I might be able to find something here."

The first little shop had puppy toys and neither of them could get past without finding a squeaky for Luna. Millie protested. "She isn't your dog; you don't have to buy her a toy."

"She spends most of the day in my shop. I can get her a toy if I want." He held up a ball. "We might even play."

Millie chose a penguin.

"She'll tear it up to get at the squeaker," Dane warned.

"Then I'll buy her another." Millie placed the stuffed toy on the checkout counter.

A few shops further, and Millie stalled, tapping the window. "Didn't you say your mother worked at a botanical garden?" It was a nature shop. She looked at Dane. He had an eye on a bird bath in the window. "Does she like stuff for the garden?"

"She even likes squirrels," he pointed, "look how they're climbing the base."

"If you get it, we can drive around to their back door. Don't think you'll want to lug that around the shops."

Dane went to check on the bird bath while Millie moved to a set of hanging chimes. She flicked her finger on a long thick tube. The low vibrating murmur didn't gain any attention. She glanced through the shop. There were a few people, along with Dane and the salesclerk. Dane had his wallet in his hand. He must be purchasing the bird bath. Millie grabbed the toggle on the chime and gently swerved into the other tubes. The full effect was louder. The clerk furrowed his brows, looking in her direction.

"Causing trouble, are we?" Dane took her arm and led her to the front. He waved at the clerk as they left.

"One must test merchandise if one is to consider its purchase." He released her as soon as they were in the main hallway, and Millie had to adjust her purse to stop herself from latching onto him. "Ah, the bath house. This is for the aunts."

Dane waved her on. "Take your time, I think I see a tinkering store ahead."

"Scaredy-cat. Would your sister or niece like anything from here?"

"I'm sure they would, but I wouldn't know where to start."

She laughed. "Go tinker. I'll catch up to you."

Millie breathed in the sweet mingle of scents as she entered the store with white fabric-draped walls. The aunts and Grandmom may be too old for baths, but they still enjoyed scented soaps and lotions. Millie found a bar for each of them and added the items to the dog bag once she paid. She made her way to the other store. She chuckled. Dane, the bookstore owner, perused a shelf of books on the back wall. He lifted a large volume and started going through the pages. She stepped beside him. "Don't you have this one?" A glossy photo of a starry sky filled both pages.

"Most of the space books I have are for the children." He turned the page.

"You can always get this for yourself for Christmas."

He closed the book. "I already have a potential Christmas present for myself."

"What do you mean, potential?"

They walked from the store as he explained. "The store actually does well because I have a large collection of rare books. Variety."

"You'll give yourself one of those for Christmas?"

"Just got one in I would love to have. But I'll stick it on the shelf for a few weeks. If it doesn't sell, it's my Christmas present to myself."

"Why not keep it?"

"I have privileges because of the bookstore. The book's value is nearly two-thousand dollars."

Millie choked. "Two thousand for a book? Are the pages gold?"

He chuckled. "It's a first edition of The Hobbit. Hard to find, unless a collector passes. Not my most valuable, but it's up there."

"There's a lot I don't know about books."

He pressed his hand to his chest. "I am an antiquarian."

"You're a book snob. Here's the retro shop for Stella." Millie waved at Ricki.

"Shop here often?" Dane asked with a grin.

"Ricki's my cousin. And yes, we shop here frequently. Hey, Ricki," Millie greeted with a hug. "This is Dane," she introduced. "He has a store downtown."

"Glad to see you know someone other than the pesky bookstore owner."

Millie made a face at her cousin as Dane's brows rose. "A pesky bookstore owner? Do tell."

Ricki stepped closer. "Word is, he tries to sabotage the bakery. You don't have trouble with him as well, do you?"

Millie sighed. "This is him, and if you don't get quiet, I'll be walking home."

Dane crossed his arms and looked back and forth between the two of them. "But I'm eager to hear more."

Ricki giggled. "You painted the window?"

Dane poked his thumb toward Millie. "Let's not forget, she turned my front stoop into a poop deck. And this was after trying to butter me up with a hot mug of cocoa."

"She does make the best hot chocolate. It isn't from a pouch."

"If you two are finished," it was Millie's turn to grumble, "I need a gift for Stella. What do you have?"

"I've got the new glasses, that's a given. You can find a dress on the back rack to match them."

"This shop does remind me of your sister," Dane commented as they walked to the rack of dresses.

"She has style," Millie agreed. "Whereas I," she looked at her outfit, "I have comfortable leggings."

'I think your legs look good in green."

His admiring look was disconcerting. She turned around to study the dresses.

He cleared his throat. "Want to get a bite to eat after this?"

"That will be good. I think this is the dress." She pulled a dress with solid white above the waist and wide red and white stripes below.

"Reminds me of Alice in Wonderland."

"She'll love it." Millie carried the dress to the counter where Ricki wrapped the glasses. She did not need to think about Dane admiring her green legs. That they could be civilized was good. There was no need for anything deeper.

Dane found himself enjoying the bit of color in Millie's cheeks. He stopped at a rack of dresses on their way out of the store. "Do you think Becky would like a dress like this? She's fourteen, I think."

Ricki pulled out a long navy dress with bands of white ruffle around the skirt. "If she's not preppy, an eclectic style like this does well. Of course, if you choose an outfit and she doesn't like it, I'll let her make an exchange."

Dane looked to Millie. She shrugged. "I think it's beautiful."

"Okay. Let me get this and then we'll go find dinner."

Dinner turned into fish-n-chips from an indoor food truck tucked away in a corner. They even had mushed peas. Dane groaned as he took a bite of fresh, perfectly cooked fish. "This is better than what I had in London."

"You've been to London?" Millie dipped one of her fries in ketchup.

"A few times, for book conventions. I've also been to Boston, Los Angeles, and Iceland."

"Iceland?" Millie laughed.

"Yes. Iceland has a strong literacy program and books do quite well."

"I would not have thought that."

"People can be surprising. Take us. After last week, who would have thought we'd be shopping together and being civil to one another?"

"You always looked grumpy. I never made an effort to get to know you."

"I do not look grumpy." He protested.

Millie smiled. "You frowned whenever I saw you."

Because she made him feel things he didn't want to feel. But he couldn't explain that to her. He could barely explain it to himself. He cleared his throat instead. "What else do you need to get?"

"A few nick knacks for the girls. Something for the aunts."

"It's a good thing I've eaten to keep my energy going."

They tossed their trash and walked along the line of shops. The old-time photo shoot gallery sparked an idea. He tapped Millie's shoulder. "Here's an unusual idea. Give them a certificate for a photo shoot after Christmas once Aunt Lettie is well enough to get around. They enjoy each other so much, and this is unique."

Millie paused in front of a photo of a group of young women standing at a bar dressed in wild west outfits. "Can you image Aunt Bea, Aunt Lettie, Grandmom Cooke, and Aunt Dahlia standing like that?"

"I'd want to come and watch. They'll be hilarious."

Millie turned to Dane. "This is the perfect idea." They studied the list of options, selecting a choice with three scenes and costume changes. Millie divided the total and bought four gift certificates. She put the thin paper bag in her purse and hugged her purse. "Do not let me lose this."

"Never. Make sure we have our other packages as well." They checked their bags, and Millie nodded.

"Any ideas for your sister?" she asked.

Dane rubbed his chin. He could feel coarse hairs. "I'm considering getting her a puppy. She's toyed with the idea, but I don't think she'll ever do it on her own."

"There's a puppy store near the back. Did you want to look here?"

"As long as it isn't a puppy farm shop."

"I think she breeds beagles, but they also take in shelter dogs that need training. Nothing spends the night on its own locked up in a cage. At least, that's what one of my customers told me. I've never checked."

"Let's go. We're almost to the back now. It can't be far."

What they found was a long store with several runs set up along with open-top cages around plastic kiddie pools. A fresh batch of four beagles yapped in one of the pools. The other pool had a gray and white mutt chewing on a stuffed Santa. Millie crouched beside the mutt. She stuck her fingers through the gate and giggled when the puppy licked her fingers.

"You know, you can reach over the top." Dane looked at the sign. "Pearl. Must be a girl."

"She's beautiful. Are you sure your sister wouldn't get mad at you?"

"If I include dog training, I think she'll love it."

"What about her husband?"

"Paul loves Sylvia. If Sylvia loves the dog, he will as well."

Millie waved at the shop keeper. "Time to find out what you'll be in for."

Pearl already had a home waiting for her. Dane felt disappointment as he walked with Millie out of the shop.

"Check in with her every few days. There's still a few weeks before Christmas." Millie suggested.

"Is it wrong to hope Pearl's plans fall through?"

"Yes," she laughed. "I'd also find a way to double check with Sylvia to make sure she's ready."

No other ideas presented themselves as they finished walking Bixby. Outside looked dark and cold. They paused near the entrance to don scarves and gloves and close their jackets.

Millie grinned at him. "Thank you for offering to shop with me. The idea for the aunts is brilliant. I can't wait to share it with them."

They walked in silence a short way before Dane spoke. "Did we just manage several hours together without fighting?"

"Um, hm. I'm pretty sure we disagreed on puppy virtues."

"Difference of opinion, not arguing."

"Well, don't expect it not to resume tomorrow."

He shot her a look. "Do you have another prank in mind?"

"No prank. I appreciate your watching Luna during the day."

"Oh," he pretended to stab himself in the chest, "I've been delegated to dog sitter."

"Do you have other talents?"

"You're using me."

The way he said it with dramatic flair made Millie giggle. "Perhaps, but you are appreciated."

Dane shook his head. "I had a good time. I still have to drive around to the nature shop for mom's bird bath."

Christmas music worked through the silence as they drove back to town. Millie gave him directions to her house. The porch and bushes were lit with blue lights.

"Looks festive," Dane commented.

"It's enough to get by. We'll set up a tree in the front window as well, this weekend."

"Maybe I'll get to see it. Have a good night."

Millie opened the door before he could get out to help. "Thank you for driving."

Dane watched as she walked to the front door. She didn't turn around or wave as she went inside. Why did he feel like it mattered?

19

Stella pulled her purse from the wooden locker. "Are you sure you'll be okay? I can wait to leave until after lunch."

Millie shook off her concerns. "We have plenty of help and we agreed you could leave today since you covered for my shopping yesterday."

"Which I haven't heard nearly enough about."

"Stories can wait until Sunday. I want something good for Christmas."

Stella waved, then went through the front of the bakery. The door jingled as she stepped into the cold. Walking along Mainstreet took her past the bookstore and a hair salon. The antique boutique had twinkling lights set up in their window display. She ignored the lights, compelled to keep walking. Both she and Millie knew the shops along Mainstreet well.

The chrome columned Mainstreet Diner wrapped the columns in garland. Hugh sat alone at a table on the other side of the window. He hadn't noticed her since he was pouring over papers and his computer, but Stella stopped. Shopping in pairs was more fun than alone. She smiled. Their last encounter hadn't been nice, and she needed to remedy that. She turned around and went into the diner.

"I need to go shopping for Christmas gifts."

Hugh frowned as she sat across from him. "What are you doing here?"

"I saw you and came inside. It's freezing out there." She noticed the pile of fries on his plate. "These look good," she said as she nabbed one. "I'm not mad at you. I figured I could enlist your help."

"What do you mean you're not mad at me? Why would you be mad at me?"

"Your lawyer friend wants to start trouble." She took another fry.

He slapped at her hand but missed. "Those are my fries. And he's not my friend. How many times do I need to explain that to you?"

"Twice. We're good now. How about you come shopping with me?"

He narrowed his eyes as he took a drink. "We haven't shopped together in ten years."

"But you're good at putting ideas together. I want to complete my list tonight."

"I don't know if that's a good idea."

Stella leaned closer. "Please?" She took another fry, grinning at his fake frown. "I'll treat you to a hot fudge sundae at Sundays."

He pulled his plate closer to his chest. "I haven't had Sundays in years. Who's on your shopping list?"

"Millie, of course. The aunts and Grandmom Cooke."

"Hm." He ate a fry, taking his time. "Perhaps we can collaborate on the aunts and grandma."

"What about heading over to the mall?"

"We're still a couple of weeks from Christmas. It

shouldn't be a complete madhouse."

Stella snatched one more fry and sat back in her seat. "Are you driving?"

"Car's parked on the street. Go order your own fries."

"Nah, I want a gyro from the food court."

Hugh made a face. "How can you eat lamb?"

Stella waited for Hugh to put his papers and computer in his leather backpack before standing. "Still harping on lamb, but cow doesn't faze you?"

Hugh held the door and they stepped outside. He pulled the collar of his blonde suede jacket after zipping it up. Stella shook her head. "We can find you a better coat while we're out and about."

"That's my plan. Grandma Keyes planned to get it for Christmas, but now she's laid up for a few weeks at least."

"Millie saw her yesterday. She and Dane visited the hospital together."

"Dane, huh? Are they an item?"

"Not according to Millie, but they seem to be getting closer. I am optimistic. Hopeful for her."

They arrived at the truck. Hugh helped Stella before getting around to the driver side. "What about you? What man do you have your sight on?"

"I am content with the status quo."

"Which means you've known everyone since grade school."

"This conversation sounds familiar. Next, you'll be telling me to head over to Minneapolis."

"I'd be run out of town if you or your sister left. The bakery's become a cornerstone."

"Which young lady do you have your eye on?"

"If I tell, it might not work out. Special cards are best kept close to the chest."

Stella groaned. "Are you still using those clichés?" She started pressing buttons on his console. "How do you turn the radio on? Let's find Christmas music."

Hugh slapped at her hand, but then obliged. Stella rode in companionable silence until Jingle Bells had them both singing. They found a decent parking spot. "Time to take this show on the road." Stella teased as they hiked to the sliding doors leading into the jumble of mall shops and kiosks.

Holiday music continued to flow around them. Giant balls in green, red, blue, silver, and gold dangled from the ceiling. An oasis of Christmas trees marked groupings of seats, many occupied with worn-looking shoppers.

"This looks festive." Hugh unzipped his jacket.

"Where do they store this much Christmas? Do they rent a storage unit or is there a basement?"

"Mainstreet could probably fit inside here. They have plenty of storage." Hugh glanced in a window with computers on display.

Stella pulled him away. "The aunts wouldn't use a computer. Did you have any ideas?"

He shrugged. "You'll think it's silly."

"What?"

He pointed down one of the hallways. "They have a shop that does monograms. They're women, purses should be well received. What about getting them the same purse, just different colors or patterns, and having them monogramed?"

"That's a great idea. We can do coordinating wallets for each of them. I think they'd love it."

It didn't take long to settle on a group of Vera Bradley purses with matching wallets. They placed their order at the monogram shop. Stella looked at her watch. "That's record time. All I need now is Millie's gift."

"What are you thinking?"

"First, kitchen store. New gadgets come out every year." Stella rubbed her hands together as they entered the store that spread through multiple rooms."

Hugh held up a tool with a long handle and a thin curved top. "Look, a cookie launcher."

Stella shook her head. "That is not a launcher. An Oreo sits on the end. You can dunk it into milk."

"It's a launcher. Check this out." Hugh put a cookie sample on the tool. He held the tool with both hands with the cookie closest to him.

Stella looked around, and then whispered. "Don't you dare."

He dared. He flung the cookie into an arch. Stella snatched it out of the air before it could hit anything.

Hugh grinned. "Good reflexes."

Stella flung the cookie back at him, hitting his chest. "Don't do that again. You'll get us in trouble."

"You're the one throwing food." He popped the cookie into his mouth.

"Keep looking." Stella picked up an icing tube.

"Looks like a kindergartener's pencil."

She pressed the button on the side and drew a design on a paper plate. "Works like one as well." The chocolate line wobbled instead of forming a clear letter.

Hugh laughed. "Looks like you've had a drink too many."

Stella grinned. "I prefer my pastry bags."

They meandered into a different section. Hugh picked up a black and white bicycle. "What's this for?"

"Tour de Pizza?" She touched the label adhered to the side. "It's a pizza cutter?"

Hugh took it back. "That is too cool. I'm getting one for myself."

"You should get one for Allison. Your sister would love it."

"Let me go grab a basket."

Hugh took off as Stella continued perusing the aisles. She picked up a turquoise ladle. Turning another corner, she gasped at an Alice in Wonderland display. "This is perfect."

"What's perfect?" Hugh returned, a basket dangling from the crook of his arm.

"This Alice apron and the matching dish towels. She could use the apron for work."

"Get what you want and stick it in the basket. What's the blue thing?"

Stella giggled. "What's this top part look like?" She held it up in front of him while hiding the base.

His brows furled as he thought. "It looks like a head with eyes, but what is it?"

Stella placed the ladle standing up on the shelf beside her.

He tilted his head. "It looks like one of those tall dinosaurs with the really long necks."

"A stegosaurus, isn't it?"

Hugh picked it up. "I'm getting one of these as well. What else did you find?"

"Nothing as unusual as that. For your sister?"

"I don't know. I might stand it up on my counter."

"What else would your sister like?"

"She's on a health kick right now."

"Nothing from the bakery, then? Oh, I saw this cool salad bowl. Back here, somewhere." Stella led Hugh back the way she had come. They went through a couple of aisles before she found what she wanted. "Here it is." The bowl came with a lid, but it had slits through the bowl.

Hugh picked it up. "How is this a salad bowl?"

"These slits make it easy to chop whatever you put in the bowl." She showed him the picture. "They have two sizes. This bigger one is good for lettuce while the smaller could work with the veggies."

"This is good. Will they nestle?" Hugh opened the bigger bowl and Stella put the smaller one inside. They closed the lid and gave it a shake.

Stella turned it upside down. "What colors? You could get them the same or choose colors that compliment."

"I think she'd like green and yellow."

"How is your other sister? She was a couple years older and I didn't keep up with her."

"She lives in New York, works in banking. That's where she met her husband, Ron. Anything else you want to get?"

"I'm getting hungry. Let's get our purchases and head over to the food court."

"With how many fries you stole, I'm surprised you have room for a gyro." Hugh led them through the maze of aisles to a set of registers near the store front.

Stella pulled her black glasses off, holding one side in her mouth as she searched her bag for her wallet.

"I take it you don't shop at the mall for yourself very often." Hugh commented.

Stella put her glasses on when she retrieved her wallet. "Why do you say that?"

"Your retro look. Which looks amazing on you, by the way. It's just not common here."

"There are several vintage shops nearby." Stella took the bag from the salesclerk. "Merry Christmas."

The clerk's smile widened when Hugh placed his items on the counter.

Stella bumped against him as they walked out of the store. "She could be a fan."

"Ha. A bit young. Food court and then look for toys for my niece?"

Stella nodded. "There's an explorer shop in the outparcel strip. They have games, puzzles, stuff like that."

"As long as it doesn't involve princesses or gnomes. Or clowns. Nothing from the clown family."

They found the Greek café and placed their order. Hugh procured a table near the fountain in the center of the food court.

Stella looked at her watch. "The purses should be ready once we finish here."

"I can't wait to see how they look."

"This is a humungous bag," Hugh laughed as they exited the embroidery shop.

"Want me to hold the other end?" Stella laughed with him. "They should make these red, then it will look like Santa's sack. Hold on." She tied a knot to make her end easier to lift. "Okay, I got it."

"We're heading directly for the car, right?"

"Lead on. Just be sure to use doors and not the swirly thing."

Hugh chuckled. "We could get stuck."

"You forget, I know how much you hate tight spaces. You'd break through and they'd charge you for damages."

He nodded. "Most expensive Christmas ever. Door it is."

They reached the car without incidence. Hugh unlocked the storage locker in the truck bed.

"That comes in handy," Stella pushed up on the tire to get a better look.

"Your jacket'll get dirty," Hugh warned as he wrapped his hands around her waist to pull her safely away.

"Dry cleaners. You think I'm being nosy." Stella pushed her glasses into place.

"You know me better than anyone. There's nothing to hide."

Stella gave him an odd look. "I haven't seen you in ten years. How well can I know you?"

Hugh helped her step into the truck. "Ten years? Why does it seem like we've done this every year since I could drive?"

She jerked her head toward the driver side. "Get a move on it cowboy." Hugh walked around the front of the truck after closing her door, and Stella hooked her seatbelt. It did feel as though no time had passed. She smiled as she nestled into the seat.

Night had settled, and the Exploratorium windows swirled with green and red. Hugh made a beeline for the telescopes.

Stella shook her head as he gazed through a series of lenses. "You said your niece is three, right?"

He looked up at her as he bent over a refracting tube. "What are you saying?"

She raised a brow. With a sigh, Hugh pulled himself to the section intended for the young crowd. He pulled up a round heavy ball with two loops across the top. "I remember these. We sat and bounced across the room.

Stella grinned. "I had a bright red one and I got mad at Millie because hers was blue and she wouldn't trade. What color do you think your niece would like?"

"Her name's Lilly. She doesn't like princess, so I assume pink is out. The purple is a pretty color." He pulled one up.

"That would be lavender."

"Same family. This is it."

"That took almost no time."

"What can I say, I know what I want. Anywhere else you want to go?"

"No, I think we have it." Stella waited as he paid for the gift. She shoved her hands in her pocket after leaving the store. Night brought colder temperatures. Hugh opened the box in the truck bed, but Stella bit her lip to keep from laughing. "I don't think it's going to fit."

"You'll have to hold it for the ride back to town."

She rolled her eyes. "I'll manage. I wonder where I can hide these gifts until we get them wrapped?" She opened the passenger door, pulled herself into the seat, and then hooked the belt before taking the large package from Hugh.

"There's plenty of storage at the mansion. I even have a craft table big enough to wrap presents on."

"You can't use that huge dining table to wrap presents."

Hugh started the truck and gave Stella a look. "The eighteen-foot mahogany table? No way. There's a square table in the butler's pantry used to prep flower arrangements. That's the table we can use."

"By we, you mean me? I remember you were all thumbs when it came to wrapping gifts."

He shrugged. "I won't object to your help."

"It may have to be late. Schedules at the bakery will be tight between now and Christmas."

"I live in the apartment. That isn't a problem for me." Hugh turned on the radio and they sang carols until they returned to Stella's house.

Stella tossed the package at him. "Thanks for letting me steal you away. I had a good time."

"You almost sound surprised."

"Let's just say I am now willing to offer a positive reference to any woman you become interested in. And I will steer you clear of anyone who is likely to become a nightmare."

"Wow. Thank you, I appreciate that, I think. I'll stop by the bakery this weekend to find out when you want to wrap."

Stella hopped out, adjusting her glasses after landing. She waved and turned toward home. The smile on her face wasn't there for any reason. She ignored the tingle.

20

Millie continued to remind herself over the next few days there was no reason to look forward to brief meetings with Dane. If one shopping trip caused flutters, best not to risk anything further. The weekend arrived. For the drive to the Christmas Gala hotel, she kept her focus on the scenery and away from thoughts of anyone else in the downtown area. Carmoon Lodge, the hotel used for the Gala, sat high on a hill east of St. Ives. The black wrought iron gates marked the entrance to the property. In the late afternoon sunlight, Millie caught glimpses of the lake sparkling like a blue jewel. Even though she'd visited the lodge several times, the beautiful old building still earned a moment of awe.

Four massive columns resembling the stately trees surrounding the lodge formed the front porch. During the summer, people lounged in stuffed chairs and couches arranged across the porch. Today, the outside area was empty. Instead of automatic doors like most modern hotels, the eight-foot wood carved doors were manned by a matched pair of greeters. Tonight, for the Christmas Gala, they were dressed as Elves.

Millie waved at Tony, the elf on the left. "Is the cart here? I have cookies and cake."

"Right inside, Miss Cooke. Let me grab it for you." Tony brought the rolling cart and helped Millie with the boxes.

"Careful with that one," Millie cautioned with a grin. "Mess up my cake and I may run out of cherry strudel for a month or two."

"Don't you worry, little miss." Tony had called her that since she was twelve and didn't seem inclined to stop anytime soon.

The lodge had an air of a mansion from a gilded age. The front hall, laid with marble, led into two front rooms. The room on the right was a sitting room. Two dozen chairs of different styles and designs were arranged in clusters of three and four. The fireplace, draped with greenery wrapped in silver ribbons, had a fire blazing, warming the room. The room to the left of the main hallway was the first dining hall. The long hand-hewn table had several groups of chairs where guests would be served refreshment with a glass of wine as they were checked into the lodge. More greenery wrapped in silver ribbons ran the length of the table. The glow of candlelight added to the charm of the room.

Millie followed Tony past the welcoming rooms, through the large sitting room and banquet hall with its wall of windows overlooking the forest and lake nestled among the hills, and out through the glass sliders onto a covered path leading to the enclosed atrium. Millie was glad to have her thick black jacket as cold nipped her nose.

The atrium at the end of the path was a blaze of light encased within glass. Warmth welcomed her as she stepped through the sliding doors. The open floor of the atrium had tall tables of various diameters arranged around a larger, central table. Tony pushed the cart to the center table, but Millie took the time to admire the glimmer of setting sun reflecting across the lake. Beautiful color filled the lake as the sun stretched beyond the hills. "Amazing," Millie breathed.

"Shall I help you set up?" Tony's question drew her back to the task on hand.

The white pavilion had a pink cast as the sun set. Millie smoothed a wrinkle from the plum-colored shimmering tablecloth covering the center table. "This is mine." The honor of the center table had her trembling. She smiled at Tony. The large box has the largest tier. "Let's get that first."

He opened and they both reached in to lift the cake and place it in the center of the round table. Millie lifted the middle tier and placed it where a pale silver circle marked the bottom. Tony had the top tier. She took it from him and set it in place. She stepped back and studied the result with a critical eye. The three tiers gave the cake good height. She adjusted the drape of the tablecloth where it brushed the floor.

"It's a beauty."

Millie beamed. "I practiced a few styles the past few weeks. This is worth the effort."

"I best return to my post, little miss." He hugged her and left.

Glass windows separated the pavilion from the cold evening. The large building decorated in plum and silver had a variety of smaller tables scattered across the white-washed pine flooring. Long thin tables lined the back wall. Millie rubbed her hands against the sides of her black tea-length dress.

"It's perfect," Gloria Phereson gasped as she drew next to Millie.

Millie fiddled with the silver locket hanging around her neck. "Do you think the cake is large enough? I should have made it bigger."

"It's beautiful. The silver is dark enough for the snowflakes to stand out. You've captured our winter wonderland theme with flare."

"Thank you for the opportunity."

"Will you stay for the Gala? The auction will be fabulous. The rooms are divine, you must have a look."

"A little while, at least. Just remember, I've been working baker hours today."

"Of course." She patted her hand. "Have a good time."

Gloria continued her course around the atrium. Millie moved to the exit leading back to the main house. Though temped to follow the path around the lodge to her car, Millie headed for the back porch. Christmas music filled the air, along with the scent of pine.

"Michelle?" a wobbly voice called. Millie had no idea she was the intended, until a hand dropped on her shoulder. "It is Michelle, isn't it?"

"Millie," she responded, then added a smile as she recognized Mrs. Mildred.

"Millie? I was close, wasn't I? How lovely to see you again."

"How is your husband? All moved in?"

Mrs. Mildred hooked arms with Millie. "Your sweet grandmother helped."

"She's my aunt."

"What, dear?"

Millie patted her arm. "No matter. What brings you here?"

"I was told it was a stunning fundraiser. Sander doesn't care for this sort of melee, but I adore them."

"Do you have friends with you to go through the rooms?"

"Of course. Beatrice will be here. I'm early." She sighed as she looked around. "I can't believe they close for this. Must lose a ton of money."

"Oh, they aren't closed. People and companies rent the rooms for a week. They decorate them however they want. During the gala, we walk around and vote on the best room."

"How does that raise money?"

"Guests vote with cash. The room with the most donations wins."

"Which room is yours?"

Millie laughed. "I couldn't afford a room here. The atrium houses an auction. I provided a cake."

"Did you? I must see it." Mrs. Mildred looped her arm with Millie.

Heating torches set along the path made the walk comfortable as Millie and Mrs. Mildred walked to the atrium pavilion. Aunt Bea wouldn't be too late. Millie left word for her to find them. They took a leisurely stroll from the house to the glassed building.

Mrs. Mildred gasped when she saw it. "They could grow roses and hot house oranges all winter in this place."

"You should visit during the day when the lake is visible."

She picked up a sheet of paper beside a basket of garden supplies. "What's this?"

"This is how you make a bid. Each line ups the value. See," she pointed at the number five in the upper left corner. "This tells how much the next line goes up."

Mrs. Mildred brushed her fingers across the list of names. "Henry is willing to pay $85 for the basket?"

Millie nodded. Mrs. Mildred wrote her name on the last line of the paper.

"Oh, no. Use the next line," Millie protested.

"Why? I think the basket is worth two hundred dollars."

Millie grinned. "Do you enjoy gardening?"

"I love toying in the soil and helping plants grow."

"Then I guess it's for a good cause."

"Is that," Mrs. Mildred shaded her eyes," I believe it is. Beatrice," she called across the room, waving her hand.

Several heads turned, but Millie recognized Aunt Bea.

Aunt Bea beamed. "Hello, girls. How good to see you," she hugged Millie and kissed her cheek.

"I've been showing Mrs. Mildred around."

"Not to the rooms?"

"Of course not."

"Very good." She moved to Mrs. Mildred. "You look stunning. Red is your color. Have you looked at Millie's creation in the center of the room? Sander said to vote on one item." Aunt Bea walked to the auction paper by the cake and signed on the next line.

"I know there are no rules against family voting, but I do hope you leave the rest of us an opportunity to auction for the cake," Gloria teased as she walked up to Aunt Bea.

The older women hugged. Aunt Bea grinned. "It's

too pretty to eat."

"I know from experience it will be more delicious than it looks." Gloria winked at Millie, and then moved on.

Aunt Bea laughed. "I swear that woman gets younger every year. She has to be eighty if she's a day, but she has more energy than I have."

Millie wrapped an arm around Aunt Bea's shoulder. "Should I call for a wheelchair?"

"Impertinent girl." Aunt Bea turned toward Mrs. Mildred who rejoined them after taking a walk to view the other items.

"I've seen too many interesting selections."

"Did you settle on one?"

Mrs. Mildred nodded. "Gardening supplies will get used." She took hold of Millie's hand. "I'm sorry dear. Your beautiful cake should go to people who will savor the treat. Not a pair of diabetics trying to get through the Christmas season."

Millie squeezed her hand. "You have nothing to worry about."

Aunt Bea admired the cake, and then turned to Millie. "Did you want to join us for a light supper before we tour the rooms, dear? Or are you meeting someone? Do you have a date?"

"No date. I'm all for supper."

Though the walk back from the atrium was slow, Millie enjoyed the company and their admiration for the lodge and its grounds. They walked further along the back porch and entered the dining hall through a glass sliding door. An elvish waiter settled them at a round table.

"Water or tea? A stronger drink?" he asked.

They all asked for cranberry tea. "Shall I fix a plate for you?" Millie offered, but they jumped at the chance to peruse the delicacies. Millie was about to dig in once everyone returned to the table, when a voice caused her heart to thump.

"May I join you ladies?" Dane's deep voice brought a flush to Millie's cheeks. She looked up. Sure enough, there he stood.

Mrs. Mildred brightened. "You haven't come for a pair of old dolls," she grinned at Millie, "I guess it's up to our Michelle to answer."

"Millie." She swallowed.

"What, dear?" Aunt Bea asked.

"Sure. Please, join us." Millie waved at the seat beside her.

He carried his plate. The tweed look had been replaced by a black suit and red dress shirt. "Thank you. These things are more fun when we enjoy the company."

"Quite a compliment," Aunt Bea elbowed Millie.

Millie felt like dropping her head on the table, but she pasted a pleasant smile on her face instead. "Did you bring a display? Or have you sponsored a room?"

"It's a display. The book tree has been such a hit, I made a small one and topped it with a gift certificate."

"What's a book tree?" Mrs. Mildred leaned in.

"Have you been to the Book Shop on Mainstreet? He built a large tree in the front window display." Millie answered for him. "The books are stacked in a circle to look like a tree."

Aunt Bea and Mildred started discussing light displays in their neighborhood. Dane leaned closer to Millie. "I noticed your cake on the table of honor.

You're talented. What flavor is it?"

"Vanilla and lemon cream with thick buttercream icing."

"I will have to order a smaller version."

"You can always order one layer instead of three tiers."

Aunt Bea glanced around the table, pulling their attention to her. "Are you ready to look at the rooms?"

"Sure." She took a last bite of a Swedish meatball. "Do you have the program?"

"What's the program for?" Mildred asked as she stood.

Dane offered her his. "People like to visit each of the rooms before making a decision. Mark the program, and at the end, tell a volunteer which room you want your donation to go to."

"Just one?"

He shrugged. "Guess you can choose as many rooms as you like."

The lodge had ten guestrooms, and each was rented. Some kept the bedroom furniture while other removed the furniture and brought a different theme for the space.

"My goodness, it's Santa," Mildred gasped. The room looked as though Santa were leaving his workshop in a loaded down sleigh.

"This would be First Bank downtown." Millie rubbed her hands on an oversized stuffed Rudolph. "They do this every year. It's become tradition."

The next room had strings of white lights draped across the ceiling above a manger scene. "This is beautiful," Millie whispered. It sounded as though crickets and sheep were nearby.

Mildred patted her hand. "It's good to keep Christ in Christmas."

Dane nodded. "They've made a simple impact. What's next?"

They stepped from the room. Aunt Bea looked at her program. "The Everlies out of Minneapolis." They stepped inside the bedroom of a pair of girls. They were tucked snug in their beds. The windows had been frosted, and a shadowy Santa crept past. Aunt Bea laughed. "You and Stella barely slept on Christmas Eve. Not until the truth of Santa Claus became known."

"We were not that bad."

Dane asked for details as they looked at other rooms. He stepped into an office. Above the figure at the desk floated a variety of fictional characters. "Oh, look. There's Dickens, and Alcott." He pointed. 'The Grinch. These are stories written with Christmas themes."

"Are you sure you didn't buy a room this week?" Millie joked.

He smiled. "This one would be mine if I could."

The hallway ended at a large room with tables where guests could discuss their choices and get the volunteers moving.

Aunt Bea sat with a sigh. "How is anyone to choose a favorite?"

"Oh," Dane showed no doubt. "Mine's the room with the author at his desk. The way they had pieces of stories hanging around …"

"I had a feeling that would be your favorite," Millie teased, "seeing how you're a book nerd."

"Guilty as charged. I'm presently lusting after a first run of The Hobbit."

Mildred seemed taken aback. "How do you lust after a book?"

"Imagine ninety years ago. Printing had style and class. High quality paper is used. Artist drawings and illustrations are included. And it's different than mass produced copies available today. Today's version was revised after Tolkien started with Lord of the Rings."

"How much is it worth?" Aunt Bea asked

"A lot." Dane turned to Millie and tapped her program. "Which room did you prefer?"

Millie didn't mind the change of topic. "Victorian Christmas. Women must have felt elegant wearing gowns."

They put their donations in envelopes and gave the envelopes to the volunteers. Millie covered her mouth as she yawned. "Excuse me."

Aunt Bea patted her hand. "You've been going since four this morning. Head home."

"I'm glad the only thing I do tomorrow is church. Stella and I can use a break."

Aunt Bea gave her a hug, and Mildred followed suit. "This has been a lovely evening. I can't wait to tell Sander all about it."

Dane shoved his hands in his pocket. "I'll walk you to your car."

"There are plenty of people here."

"Humor me."

"Fine."

They walked to the front hallway to retrieve their coats. Millie felt her heart skip a beat when Dane took her coat to help her. "Thank you," she offered a brief smile.

"I hope you didn't mind my joining you and your

aunt for the evening."

She hesitated a moment. "I enjoyed the evening more than I thought I would."

Dane took a deep breath as they walked outdoors. "Still, I think I want more. Be my date to the Christmas concert next Friday night."

Millie stumbled, and he steadied her with a hand to her elbow. She cleared her throat. "Date?"

"Yes, date. Not an accidental meeting. Not a nondate. A date, date."

"What kind of concert is it?"

He waved at the lit Christmas tree in the front yard. "Christmas. It'll be fun, you'll see."

"Okay." Millie couldn't believe she was agreeing. "I'll go to the concert with you."

"And have dinner beforehand."

"You're pushing your luck." She forced herself to frown.

"You've said yes once. Might as well go for two."

Millie raised a brow as she put her hand on the car door. "This could prove disastrous."

He opened the door for her, then cocked his head and offered a grin she never expected from him. The giddy feel did not fade as she drove away, refusing to watch through the rear-view mirror to see if he stood and watched as well. Had she agreed? At the first stop, car stilled, she screeched and bumped her head against the steering wheel. What was she thinking?

***

What was he thinking? Dane couldn't stop the grin as he returned to the party once Millie's taillights disappeared from view. Sure, they could get along. Most human beings could. Why ask her out? Why give the tease that brought a red flush across her cheeks and made her eyes sparkle?

"I've seen that look a time or two," Mildred tapped his arm a few times.

Dane jerked his attention back to the gala fundraiser. "What look?"

"Falling in love, of course."

Dane coughed. "I'll settle for not being enemies. My life is good as is. I don't need any complications."

She laughed. "As if the heart cares about things like that."

Aunt Bea returned with two coats. Dane helped her into the long faux fur and then assisted Mildred with her puffed royal blue. "Thank you, ladies, for allowing me to be your escort for the evening. I enjoyed myself."

Aunt Bea hugged him. Once he got over the initial surprise, he hugged her back. She gazed up at him. "I think I will be seeing more of you, young man."

Dane swallowed. There was no purpose for their pointed thoughts. He'd already asked Millie to the concert, but there was no reason to anticipate anything else, this Christmas season or ever.

21

"Ah, hah, there you are little bugger." Stella cried out as she tapped the computer monitor. Luna jumped to her feet with a bark, and then flopped back against the couch cushion. A few moments later, bare feet padded down the stairs. A bleary-eyed Millie came into view in the doorway to their home office.

"What are you doing?" Millie yawned. "Do you realize what time it is?"

Stella stopped twirling her pen. "Not that late," she glanced at the lower righthand corner of the monitor. "Oh. What happened to midnight?"

Millie glared, then scooped Luna into her arms. "Go to bed." She stomped out.

Stella tugged on her fingernail with her teeth. She wasn't tired. Maybe Hugh still had a few night owl tendencies. She sent him a text. *Sleeping beauty or Dracula?*

In less than a minute, her phone chirped. *The cold grave can wait until dawn.*

She grinned. *Meet me at the square in town.*

As you wish.

Stella wrapped a scarf around her neck and slipped into her coat. She grabbed her purse and quietly opened and closed the front door. Cold tapped on her nose. Although walking to the town square would only take twenty minutes, it was the middle of the night and Stella chose to drive. The blue Volkswagen bug wasn't as practical as Millie's SUV, but it got great mileage. Plus, it was fun to drive and quiet to boot. Stella pulled into the street and drove at a normal pace. Hugh would need longer to drive in from the mansion. "I am sneaking out to meet up with an old boyfriend in the middle of the night." Her summation in the rearview mirror made her smile. She hadn't thought of Hugh in years.

She parked in front of town square, turning her lights off and waiting for Hugh to arrive. A pair of headlights turned onto Mainstreet. The tree in the square glowed. Lampposts on each of the corners were bright. Stella could see Hugh get out of his truck still wearing his suede jacket. She got out and caught up with him. "Haven't upgraded to a real coat yet?" she teased.

Hugh put on leather gloves. "You're jealous. Suede is sweet." He rubbed his right hand over his left sleeve.

Stella skipped closer and bumped him. "You're goofy."

"I'm not the one texting at 2 in the AM."

"You answered."

Snapping back and forth reminded her about who they had been in high school. Stella moved to the swings. "I'm glad they kept these when they revamped the play area." She kicked forward and felt herself lift. She pulled back to go the other way.

Hugh sat beside her, swinging with his feet on the ground. "Not much has changed in ten years." He swung to the right to bump her out of place. "Not even you."

"Hey, watch it, buster."

"Why are you up late?"

She shrugged. "End of the week. Millie went to the gala tonight, but I was trying to figure out a discrepancy between our bank summary and my computer program."

"We know you love puzzles."

She swung her legs to go higher. "Couldn't step away until I solved it. Millie was home and in bed by that time."

"Which is where you should be.

"Bakery's closed tomorrow and I can crash."

"What about lunch at Grandmom's after church?"

"I like lunch at Aunt Lettie's, she has a dishwasher."

Hugh laughed. "As good a reason as any to join us."

Stella slowed, twisting from side to side as she leaned against the chain. "I appreciate a good home cooked meal."

He tapped her boot with his. "Then it's time to get home and get to bed."

She stood and stretched. "Tell Aunt Lettie we'll see her tomorrow."

**

Hugh wanted to wrap his arms around Stella, but she showed no signs of seeing him as anything other than old business. "I'm making cinnamon coffee cake. You don't have to bring anything."

"You are making desert?" Stella acted surprised.

Hugh kept pace with her to her car. "I have basic skills."

She grinned. "I guess things have changed in ten years."

"Ha." He jabbed her shoulder, and then opened her car door for her. "Nice car. I bet it could almost fit under my truck."

"Doing my part to save the planet." She got in and gazed up at him. "See you later."

"Alligator," he said as he shut the door for her. Was she torturing him on purpose? He walked to his truck. She waited until he was in and had started the vehicle. He followed her home even though she would not appreciate the gesture. With a sigh, her car parked in the driveway, he headed out of town to the Ives Mansion.

22

Sunday afternoon, Luna's tail whooshed back and forth as Millie knelt to unhook the leash. After shaking her head, Luna raced across the field.

'Wow, I didn't realize she was that fast."

Millie jumped at the sound of Dane's voice. 'What are you doing here?" She looked around the fenced dog park.

Dane pointed across the park at the jogging trail. "A brief stint above freezing with the sun shining? I'm all over this park. I thought I heard a familiar bark and came to investigate."

He wasn't the only one to recognize a voice. Luna raced back at them, jumping with an excited yelp.

"Luna," Millie laughed, grabbing hold of the collar while trying to keep her grounded.

Dane crouched and rubbed the dog's head. "How are you doing, girl?"

"Don't encourage her. She shouldn't jump."

"It wasn't a jump. She was saying hello."

Millie shook her head. "You're the reason she sits on our feet under the dining room table trying to beg for food."

He stood, holding his hands up. "Not me. I don't

even have a dining table in the shop."

"Not true," Millie said, watching Luna race away once more.

"Is this why she's well behaved at the store?" Dane stood beside her.

Millie tried not to notice his pleasant smell. "I've managed to bring her a few times. Stella runs her around the park, too."

"What about tomorrow?"

"We'll be open every day but Sundays from now until Christmas Eve, but I should be able to break around eight to bring her over."

"There's a park across the street from our shops, behind the library. How about we meet there? The park has a fence and if we go early, there shouldn't be people. Give Luna a chance to run off steam."

"We haven't needed to do that the past couple of weeks. Why start now?"

"She's a growing dog. She's already five pounds bigger than when you first found her."

"She is growing," Millie agreed, fighting the urge to refuse because it meant spending more time with Dane. There was nothing wrong with Dane. At least, no reason why he should make her nervous. "Okay, fine. Eight tomorrow. I'll bring Luna to the other park."

"I'll see you in the morning." Dane watched for a moment, going from Millie, to Luna, and back to Millie. With a slight grin, he jogged off the way he'd come.

The sunshine of the previous day gave way to overcast skies and cold. Millie secured her scarf into the top of her coat. Even with ears wrapped, she was still cold. "What am I doing here?" she muttered, looking across the park at the glow of sunrise. Luna gave a bark of encouragement. "I should have just left you with Aunt Bea today," she muttered as she unhooked Luna's leash. The dog sniffed at the frozen ground, crouched over a spot, and then raced away.

"Don't go too far," Millie hollered. "I can't see too well."

"Did you make sure the gate on the other side was closed?" Dane stepped beside her blowing into his hands.

"Gate?" Millie looked across the park. "What gate? Luna," she called. "Look who's here."

Dane gave a whistle and the wiry dog bounded to them. He crouched beside her, rubbing her head. "Good job, Luna. Good listen. You're a smart girl, aren't you?"

Millie took advantage of Luna's attention on Dane and hooked her back on the leash. "You are a smart girl, aren't you?" She rubbed the dog's side.

Luna bounced up to lick Millie's nose, then danced around her. Millie tried to turn to keep the leash from tangling around herself and Dane, but the dog moved faster. With a last-ditch effort to keep from falling, she grabbed Dane's coat. His hands looped around her waist, but the leash had twisted around their legs. Millie gave a cry as they tumbled to the cold ground. Luna jumped over them, barking. Dane grunted, hitting the ground first, and then again as Millie landed on top of him.

She felt heat infuse her cheeks as she rolled off him. "I'm so sorry. Are you okay? We didn't hurt you, did we?" She sat up, pulling the leash away from their feet. Luna continued to dance around them as Dane sat up laughing. Millie watched him, enjoying the sound.

He grabbed hold of Luna, unhooking her. "I'll hold her while you make sure we're no longer tangled."

Millie gave herself a mental shake. There was nothing interesting about Baxter Dane. No reason why she should feel uncomfortable by him. "I'm sorry," she apologized once more before pulling in the remaining length of leash and pushing herself to her feet. "Here, I've got her now." She wrapped the leash around her hand to allow no slack once Luna was set down. She leaned down to hook her again.

"You should get one of those retracting leashes."

Millie offered her empty hand to help Dane stand.

"Thanks."

His slow grin made her insides tumble. She tried to focus on the happy dog. "I have to get back to the bakery."

"I have plenty of time before I need to get to the shop. How about I run her around a bit more?"

"Are you sure? You won't be out here too long? It's getting colder." Morning had brightened, but the sky remained overcast. Cold fingers of wind touched Millie's neck where her scarf had fallen away.

"We'll be fine." Dane took her scarf, wrapped it around her neck, and tucked the ends into the top of her coat. "I'll walk a lap with her, and we'll head for the shop. We'll all be warm and cozy in no time."

Millie relinquished the leash without a comment. Her thoughts were still fumbling around the feel of his knuckles brushing against her neck.

Dane tilted his head. "You okay?"

"Yes." Millie forced a smile. "The cold makes my brain fog up. I'll see you this afternoon." She turned and walked away. What was with her? Dane was kind. Much more than she'd thought he could be. They could be friendly neighbors. There was nothing else. Except for the date on Friday.

Millie hummed as she arranged the final tray for the window display. The first shelf had been removed to make room for the gingerbread house. The other Christmas cookies were old-fashioned delights. The meringues had a golden hue on their curls. Thumb prints were grape, strawberry, or marmalade. Peanut butter kisses came out perfect.

"Millicent. How nice to see you. Thought you might have French macaroons, but I see I was mistaken." Nora breezed into the bakery.

Millie stood. "I prefer classic recipes."

"Of course, you do. You would require real training for complex recipes like the French have."

Millie tried not to think about her Mrs. Claus apron over her black pants and T-shirt, or the fact her make-up had melted away hours ago. Nora's make-up and hair looked fresh, even if her three-inch boot heals were impractical for Mainstreet, St. Ives. "I wouldn't mind a visit to Paris someday, but my focus today is the bakery."

"And a certain bookstore owner a few doors down?"

"What do you mean?"

"I saw the two of you this morning with the dog. It's good to see Dane smiling again. The death of his wife hit hard."

"Wife?" Millie struggled to breath.

"Yes. A sweet woman, taken from him too soon. There were many nights I listened to him talk about her.

I admit," Nora held her hand to her throat. "I fell in love with him, but it wasn't the time to do anything about it."

"I had no idea."

"Why would you? Now I see he's able to smile and laugh again, I can show him my interest." She waved a finger at Millie. "You aren't interested in him as well, are you?"

"Me? Of course not. We're barely friends."

"Not sure why I thought otherwise." Nora laughed. "Dane is a sophisticated man, what would you have in common?"

"A book worm and a baker? Not much at all, I agree." The lightness of her heart slipped away.

"I need to finish shopping. Happy holidays." As fast as she'd come, Nora was gone. Millie wished she could rewind to before the visit, but her spirits sank lower.

"Was that Nora Wentworth? What was she doing here?" Stella wiped her hands on her apron.

"Insulting the quality of my baking." Millie swept past her sister. "We aren't French enough for her."

Stella followed. "Do not let Miss Priss ruffle your feathers. You love the way you bake. Plenty of others do as well."

"Have you seen the green drinks she carries around with her?" Millie made a face. "I wouldn't trust her taste anyhow."

"Something she said upset you." Stella waited, but Millie refused to give in to the whirlwind of emotion.

"I'm going to get cleaned up and get Luna. I think a long hot soak in the tub is in order tonight."

"Then I'll see you at home. I think Hugh is stopping by the café this afternoon." Stella paused, her hand on the door between the café and kitchen and faced Millie. "Whatever Nora said, take with a grain of salt. She wasn't honest when we knew her in school, and I haven't seen anything to make me change my mind now."

"Thanks, sis." Stella had a good point. A shimmer of hope sparked. She wanted to agree with Stella, but why hide he had a wife? It didn't make sense, and until she understood, Nora's comments seemed plausible. Which meant broken heart. "Oh, no." She reassured herself. "There is nothing broken here."

Millie felt more like herself as she walked from the bakery to the bookstore. She got into the store without seeing Dane. Hopefully, she could leave with Luna and not see him at all.

But her luck didn't hold. "Got a hot date you're running off to?" Dane stood in a doorway.

"A hot bath is more like it."

"That's not a place my thoughts need to go."

Millie felt her cheeks burn. "Of course not, nor should they. I prefer hot baths fully clothed, nothing indecent."

He laughed, then sobered. "If I've made you uncomfortable, I apologize. I didn't mean to."

"I'm not uncomfortable."

"They why won't you look at me?"

She did and gave him a quick smile. "I was focused on the dog. It's not you."

"Feels like its me."

"Talk with Nora. She'll make you feel better."

"Nora? What does she have to do with this?"

"Nothing, at least not with me. You are free to like whomever you want."

"I thought it was obvious who I was starting to like."

"Nora told me about your wife. About how she consoled you. She's ready to let your relationship mature."

He sighed and rubbed the back of his neck. "I planned to tell you about my wife."

"You did? At least I assume she's the one who went away and left you a dog."

"My wife's name was Rebecca. She and Nora were good friends. I was young and impetuous, and it turns out, nothing what Rebecca wanted in her husband. We were divorcing, and yes, I was keeping the dog. Her death was a tragic accident."

"But Nora said—"

"I don't care what Nora said. I have never been interested in her. I'm interested in you."

He kissed her, and confusion took a back seat. Millie dropped Luna's leash and wrapped her arms around Dane because she felt unbalanced. "It's not a third date," she tried to protest as he teased her lips.

"What's that supposed to mean?"

"We should go on three dates before... well," Millie didn't seem to mind when he kissed her again.

"We'll consider this practice for the real thing." His voice was husky.

"Where's the dog?" Her voice squeaked a little.

"We should find Luna," he agreed, but neither of them moved.

A crash came from the next room. Millie pulled back. "That didn't sound good."

Dane released her. "Luna?" He cleared his throat and called a little louder. The golden terrier raced into the room, sitting in front of them, her tail wagging. "What did you do?" Dane frowned.

Luna's tail slapped harder against the floor. Millie giggled. "I don't think she's worried. We best try to find what fell."

They moved toward the front of the shop. Luna ran around them, hopped onto a chair, and up to the table where the book tree had been.

"Oh, no." Millie looked at the jumble of books on the floor and across the table. "Luna!"

"Seems trouble thinks she's a cat." Dane sighed.

Millie knelt, stacking a few books and winding up garland. Luna jumped between her arms. "You are not helping." She glanced at Dane. "Put her in her cage and we'll get this fixed."

"You don't have to worry about it." He picked up the dog.

Millie added another book to the stack. "I said I'd clean up any messes she made."

"You did promise, didn't you?" Dane carried the dog away.

By the time they finished fixing the book tree, night had fallen. Millie watched a few flakes falling outside the window. "I think it's going to be dinner and a short bath." Millie leaned over to pick up Luna.

"Do you want to go out the back?"

"Good plan." She gave him a quick smile. "We'll see you tomorrow."

"Still on for dinner and the concert Friday? First official date?" Dane held the back door for her.

Millie tilted her head. "Disaster may strike."

"I think we'll be good. I'll pick you up at your place." Luna barked. "Not you," Dane shook his head, "just Millie."

"Okay, great." Millie muttered, walking away. Jittery nerves made her want to giggle, but she bit her lip. Had he kissed her? He kissed her. Dane kissed her. Millie kissed him back. Now what?

23

Wisps of white blew through the dark of predawn. Millie wrapped her scarf securely around her neck, ignoring the shiver making her want to return to the warmth of her bed. Though it wasn't snowing, the moist air could cause ice on the roads, especially the bridges. "At least we don't have raised overpasses like the city," she conversed with herself. No one else was on the road yet. No one would complain she kept the speedometer a few degrees below the speed limit. She turned onto Mainstreet. Two blocks shone with light from the streetlamps. In the strong glow nearest the lamps, there appeared to be flurries drifting among the fog. "As long as we aren't drenched in feet of snow," Millie whispered to the quiet. Nothing disturbed her as she parked, waited for Uncle Doe, and then opened the bakery.

She moved into her familiar routine, preparing fresh goods for the day. Once she had the trays full, she could begin the stack of specialty orders. Stella joined her as she dribbled icing on crullers. Stella unhooked her gray and white checkered jacket. "This fog 'll make it a slow morning."

Millie switched to chocolate drizzle. "I checked the

weather channel. Nothing about snow or ice. We should be good once the sun gets up."

"Later and later every day, lazy sun." Stella teased as she wrapped an apron around her green and white dress. "What am I starting on?"

"There's a box of sugar cookies from yesterday afternoon. You can get those prepped and placed."

"On it, boss."

Millie finished the donuts and placed them in the glass display behind the counter. Stella hadn't returned from the back closet. Millie went in search of her. "Everything okay back here?"

Stella held a clipboard in her hands while checking between a label on one of the boxes and papers on the clipboard. "I've never even heard of Cherno's before."

"What is it?" Millie moved closer.

"Angela checked in the order yesterday. Did you call for a new brand?"

"Our spices and sugar all come from Benino's. We wouldn't use a different brand."

"Look, none of this is what you would order." Stella handed her the clipboard.

Millie looked at the list. What was going on? She placed the order herself a week ago. This wasn't right. "Let me call dispatch. That other stuff won't work, we have to have Benino's."

"I'll finish the muffins. I've got a gingerbread chocolate chip I want to try."

"Those would be good as minimuffin baskets."

Millie walked to the office of the bakery. In keeping with the character of the place, the room had a deep gray paint above tall white wainscoting. Shelves for storage and two filing cabinets lined one wall. The oak desk sat toward the center of the room. Millie sank into the chair, leaning back and listening for the familiar squeak. She slid open the left top drawer and pulled out her smartphone. She scrolled through contacts until she saw the supply company. With a push, she watched the blue line shift across the screen. The phone jangled as the call went through.

"Lacie Montgomery, may I help you?"

"This is Millie Cooke with Bake-n-Cake."

"Good morning, Miss Cooke. How are you?"

"A bit confused. Stell and I were just checking the inventory that came in yesterday. None of our usual brand is there."

"Let me look." She paused for a moment, and then continued. "You placed the order last week. I have your name with it."

"But I didn't order Cherno's. I've never heard of them before."

"Of course not. That's more like a brand substitute. You've always stuck with Benino."

"Why was Cherno delivered yesterday?"

"It was? Hold on, I see. Kim took a change in order the next day. A man made the change."

"A man? Who? I don't have any men working for me at this time."

"I'm not sure. I'll have to find out from Kim why that information is missing. She should have taken down his contact information and then connected with you to recertify the order."

"You'll have to pick this up and get my proper order. How soon?"

"Let me check. I'll have to get back to you. Are you sure you don't have a man working there? We have protocols in place to prevent mishaps and pranks."

Millie hated that her thoughts turned to Dane. He would never do anything to disrupt business or hurt the quality of their baked goods. Other thoughts of him were too distracting. She focused on her conversation with Lacey. "Alright, let me know as soon as you can. I'm going to need those supplies tomorrow."

Millie leaned back in the chair and looked at the photo of their parents hanging on the wall. "We've been here three years, and it took this long to get a faithful following. I'm not going to allow anyone to mess that up."

"Mills, you better get out here. What is going on today?"

Millie jumped to her feet. Stella stood at the counter watching a stranger poke at the drains in the sink. "Hello?" Millie stepped closer to the strange man.

"Good morning. I gave my card to your coworker."

"I'm the owner, Millicent Cooke." She held her hand toward him. He reluctantly shook hands. "Are you an inspector?"

"I am."

"We have our forms displayed in the café as well as the kitchen."

"Good. Your regular inspector will be pleased to note that. I'm here because a complaint was lodged."

"A complaint?" Millie looked at Stella. "If it has something to do with Leticia Keyes falling, that wasn't on our property."

He gave her a cold look. "A customer fell?"

Stella frowned. "There was an accident out near the street, but a lawyer threatened to cause trouble."

"I am unaware of that incident. This is regarding

misuse of materials. Are you cutting corners, Miss Cooke?"

"Cut corners? We cut cookies. For the bakery."

"I'll need an inventory list."

Millie felt her stomach drop. "Yesterday's delivery was wrong. I've already called about it."

"What do you mean, wrong?"

Millie led him to the storage room. "These boxes with the red Cherno labels are not our usual product."

"Do you stock the wrong products on your shelves?"

"Angela took the delivery. She had the list from them. I can show you on my computer what was ordered."

"And you say you've already called about it?"

"Yes. I spoke to Lacie Montgomery. She's my usual supplier. She claims a man called the day after I placed the order. The girl who took his call didn't get the contact information like she should have."

"How much of this product have you used?"

"None. I'm not planning on using any of it either."

He examined the shelves for a minute. "I'll need to check the inventories. I won't have anything to cite you for if none of these boxes have been opened."

"Of course. We just discovered the mistake this morning." His contemplation made Millie feel like a wayward school child. "We'll leave you to check the inventory. I'll make a copy of the order I placed."

Stella followed her to the office. "What is going on?" she whispered, checking the door. "A mysterious man changes our order with the supplier and then calls for an inspector?"

"If I find out who it is, he'll have a shoe-sized dent

in his skull." Millie punched keys to bring up the order that should have been delivered.

"It can't be Dane."

"Of course not." Millie ignored the wayward thoughts suggesting it could be. "This person is being mean. Like leaving a dog in the cold to freeze kind of mean."

"Why would he do this to the bakery?"

"I have no idea." The printer on the locked file cabinet beside the desk completed its print job. Millie stacked the pages together and stapled them. The question remained, why. She had a feeling the lawyer might have something to do with it.

The inspector left after receiving the invoice papers, along with Lacie's contact number. Angela arrived as Millie finished swirling tops for cupcakes. She glanced at the clock. A little after ten. She undid her apron. "Stells, did you drop Luna at the Book Shop?"

Stella popped her head through the door between the kitchen and the café. "Yes, why?"

"I'm going to take her for a walk."

"Do not even think of blaming this on Dane."

"I won't. I know he's not involved. Taking Luna for a walk will help clear my head."

Stella grinned. "Seeing Dane will help clear your head."

"You're hopeless," she laughed as she threw a towel at the door. It was already closing.

Still, she heard Stella. "Not as hopeless as you."

"Brat."

The morning's fog had cleared. Millie, wrapped in her black jacket, gloves, and scarf, felt the knot that had formed through the morning fade. She skipped up the steps to the Book Shop. Dane sat at a table with a teenager. Memory of their meeting the previous day caused her cheeks to heat. She waved as she went through. Luna, upon hearing footsteps, went from wagging tail striking the wood floor, to sitting up and sweeping her tail from side to side as she watched Millie approach. "Hello, girl," Millie cooed as she bent to rub Luna's head.

"Hello yourself." Dane surprised her.

She turned. "Good morning. I didn't mean to pull you from a customer."

"Not to worry," he turned and waved at the young woman to join them. "This is my niece, the one I told you about."

"Becky?"

The young woman nodded, her smile widening. "Hey."

Streaks of blue through her hair made it difficult to compare uncle and niece. Millie offered her hand. "Nice to meet you. How's your friend doing?"

"She's coming back to school after Christmas break. She's in full remission."

"That's wonderful! Your uncle thought you might like to bake cookies with me at the bakery."

"You're from Bake-n-Cake? I would love to get a cooking lesson from you. Can Lindsey come too?

"If she's feeling up to it, it would be fun to have you both. How about Sunday afternoon? We aren't open. I can work with the two of you for a few hours. Maybe invent a new recipe."

Dane rubbed Becky's head. "Use a touch of food coloring and call it the blue dazzle."

"Hey, I like the blue," she giggled as she ducked

under his arm. "What time Sunday? I want to call Lindsey."

"Two o'clock. We can wrap up around five. If you haven't gorged on cookies, maybe we'll stop for pizza afterwards."

"I can meet you for pizza and take the girls home." Dane offered as he took a step closer. "I'll see you Sunday. Maybe I can find an excuse to see you Saturday."

"The following week will be Christmas," Millie swallowed, fighting the silly smile she felt certain graced her face. "We'll all be super busy."

"Hard to believe, isn't it?"

Millie shook her head. "Christmas took forever when I was young. Now, I wish I had half that much time."

"Bakery's not busy this morning?" Dane asked.

"Probably is now. I needed a few minutes to clear my head." Millie frowned. "An inspector came in right before we opened. They got a tip."

Dane held up his hands. "I had nothing to do with it."

Millie waved off his protest. "I know it wasn't you. The weird thing is, a man changed our order last week and the wrong supplies were delivered yesterday. If any of those packages had been opened, we could have been fined."

Dane frowned. "That's serious. What's going on?"

"I have no idea. I just keep hearing that lawyer, JT, saying there would be trouble."

Dane did something that surprised her. He wrapped his arms around her and allowed her to rest her head on his shoulder. She breathed, liking his scent. The thought startled her, and she pulled away, tucking her hair behind her ear as she stared at the floor. Yesterday's kiss played in her mind. How easy would it be to tilt her head...?

"Since sleeping beauty is awake, why don't we run her outside?"

"Great idea." Millie reached for the leash at the same time as Dane. She jerked at his touch.

He placed his hands on either side of her face. "You are unbalancing my life."

"I doubt that."

"Why are you jumpy?"

"Luna's jumpy. She wants to go out."

"What if I want to stay here?"

"I have a three-date rule. Third dates the charm, and we haven't had a first date yet."

"Shopping."

She shook her head, and he dropped his hands.

"The Christmas Gala."

"That was unplanned coincidence."

He grabbed the leash and attached Luna. "I'm counting them anyway. That makes cookie and pizza Sunday the charming number three."

"No, it doesn't," Millie tried to protest, but he was already walking away, Luna on his heels. From the butterflies swarming inside of herself, the idea of Sunday being date number three wasn't a bad idea. She groaned as she followed them.

Dane plodded down the steps. Luna sniffed at the lamp post near the street. "Dead grass is over here, girl." Dane shivered as he spoke.

Millie laughed. "It's freezing."

He pushed out his chest. "I'm a man. I can take it."

She lifted her brows as he began to shake. "You can take this cold?"

"Here, hold this."

Millie took the leash, then squealed as Dane stood behind her and pushed his hands into her pockets. "You can't do that. Those are my pockets."

"Sharing is a good thing. Don't let go of the dog."

His arms were wrapping around her and she was not cold. "I'm not letting go of the dog. You need to let go of me. What will people think?"

"That you're a good friend."

"I'm glad you think of me as a friend. Get inside before you freeze."

He shivered. "Okay, I think you're right. Here." He handed her the doggy bag from the pocket. He pointed. "I think you've got Luna muffins to clean up." He left before she could ask him to take care of it.

"Uh huh, manly." She loved on Luna for a moment. "Good girl." Cleaning up the mess was easy, and the nearby trashcan meant she didn't have to take the special package into the bookstore. Dane was helping a patron when she went back inside. Becky found her closing the door on Luna.

"I talked to Lindsey and Sunday works."

"I'm glad. I'll see you then. Have your uncle bring you to the back door."

"He's a good guy."

Millie tilted her head, peaking at Dane walking with an older man in a different room. "I'm still deciding."

Millie smiled as she returned to the bakery.

Stella handed her a cake order. "Can we get this done by the 24th?" She leaned back and studied her sister. "What are you up to?"

"Me? Nothing. All is good." Millie looked at the cake order. "A wedding cake in less than 2 weeks? And the one next Tuesday."

"I told the girl it may not be possible, but you were also a miracle worker."

"Yeah, right. Maybe Becky and Lindsey would like to see a wedding cake get decorated."

"Who are Becky and Lindsey?"

Millie handed the note back to Stella. "Call and say we can do it. Becky is Dane's niece. She made the cookies Dane was selling."

"To raise funds for her sick friend."

"Yes, Lindsey. She's getting better. I promised Becky a baking lesson and Becky asked if Lindsey could come as well."

"When?"

"Sunday."

"I'll come help with the cake."

Millie checked her nails and rubbed them against her shirt. "We're going for pizza after we finish."

"You and the girls? They'll like that."

"And Dane. He has to pick them up. Seemed right to invite him."

Stella's face lit. "I will join you as well. Will be interesting to see how you behave when you aren't at each other's throat."

24

Late afternoon, cold wind seeped through the air, chilling Millie as she struggled to unlock the front door of her home with her hand still encased in a mitten. Luna danced beside her. With a grunt of frustration, Millie pulled the mitten off with her teeth and turned the key in the lock. She pushed the door closed as soon as she was through and leaned against it to catch her breath. She released Luna from her leash and dug the stack of mail out of her pocket before pulling the coat off.

"I'm moving to Florida."

Luna barked in agreement.

Millie fished through the mail on the table. There were the usual coupon pages, a local magazine, and a few Christmas cards with familiar names on the return address label. There was also a long envelope with an embossed logo. Reynolds and Beane? Why did that name sound familiar?

Millie grabbed the letter opener from the desk in the next room. She sliced through the linen-quality envelope and pulled out a short stack of papers stapled together. The jargon on the papers made little sense. Millie found the name of the bakery as well as her and

Stella's names. The name of the building owner was listed on page three. What was going on? She skimmed through the rest of the pages, but it didn't make sense.

Millie pulled Luna into the bathroom. "I'm sorry girl, I'll be back soon. You'll be okay." The forlorn look she received as she closed the door didn't sway Millie to take Luna with her. She grabbed her purse and the documents and strode from the house.

Cold struck like a slap to the face, but she didn't go back for her coat. She jogged to the car and turned the heat high. Second thoughts crowded her head, but there was a parking space in front of the bookstore. Before she could persuade herself otherwise, she ran from the car to the store.

A fire was going, and she took a moment to warm her hands before going in search of Dane.

"Hey, I didn't expect to see you."

She turned at the sound of his voice.

"What's the matter?"

She held the papers toward him. "Does this make sense to you? It seems like the building owner is trying to break our lease agreement."

"Break the lease?" He took the papers. "Why would they do that?"

"How can they do that?"

"My sister's a lawyer. Let me have her look at it."

"I've met Mr. Carmichael on several occasions and he's always been cordial. This doesn't seem like him at all."

"We'll figure this out when we know more."

"I'm sorry, I shouldn't have barged in like this."

"It's closing time."

"Which means you have plenty to do. Don't worry

about this." Millie reached for the papers.

Dane stopped her with a hand against her cheek. "I'm glad your first instinct was to come here. I care about you, which means I care about your sister and the bakery."

"Why do you care? We've harassed each other for ages."

"I guess we've been fighting this from the beginning."

He waited for a retort, but Millie couldn't think of one. She finally waved her hand. "Maybe." The legal papers sat on a table beside them. "You think your sister can help?"

"Yes, I believe she can." His hand moved to her hair, twisting a lock around his finger.

With a deep breath, Millie stepped back. "Becky comes to the bakery tomorrow. You'll see her mom then?"

Dane grinned. "Yes, I'll give this to Sylvia in the morning."

"Stella's coming with us for pizza. Might as well see if Sylvia wants to come along as well."

"Dinner is turning into a party. At least I'll have you to myself next Friday night."

Millie tilted her head. "Friday night? Stella and I are having our hair done at the beauty shop."

"Uh, huh. I've never had a date wear a salon cape, but I don't mind firsts."

"I'll tell her to use her most dazzling. I'm sure she has a few eye-turners."

"Get out of here. I'll see you tomorrow with the kids."

Millie scooted. "Don't lose those papers." She

yelled before heading out the front door. She ran for the car, surrounded with cold and giggles.

Becky arrived with Lindsey a few minutes before one Sunday afternoon. Millie met them at the back door of the bakery, waving to Dane in his SUV. He tapped his watch and Millie showed him five. With a thumb's up, he drove away.

Millie ignored the flustered feeling and turned to her guests. "I hope you come ready to help. We just received a large order from the Rec Center for this week, along with a wedding cake."

Becky's mouth dropped. "We're helping with refreshments for the Snow Drop Run?"

"And a real wedding cake?"

Millie locked the door. "If you're okay with that."

"Okay?" Becky looked at Lindsey. Both girls nodded with enthusiasm.

"Let's bake." She showed them where to hang their coats and hats. Lindsey kept a mauve knit cap on her head. She was pale and thin, but her large brown eyes sparked with mischief.

"Bring the industrial mixer to the island. It has wheels to roll across the floor."

Millie showed them how to use the large measuring sets, as well as when to add a special pinch for flavor. She had them smell the semi-sweet chocolate chips, then a variety of spices to find what would complement the chocolate flavor. With the first few batches of chocolate chip cookies baking, she let them play with mocha and expresso flavors.

With cookies baking and cooling, Millie brought three sheets of vanilla cake that would be used to create the wedding cake. "I baked these yesterday. We cool the cake to make it firm for working with."

Lindsey scratched a spot on her head through her cap. "When is the wedding?"

"Tuesday. Today we'll shape and do the base icing. That leaves tomorrow to put it together and add the details." Millie moved to the counter. "Pull the small mixer over here."

Stella arrived as Millie had the girls measuring ingredients for lemon cream filling. Millie waved her over. "Perfect timing. You want to help Lindsey mix the lemon filling while Becky and I cut the cake layers?"

Stella agreed. Millie led Becky to the island.

"Why don't you use different sized pans to form your cake?" Becky asked.

Millie pulled out the drawing for Becky to see. "We get more cake this way. Arrange these plastic circles on the pans. Make sure nothing overlaps."

Becky took the challenge, giving each piece a serious study as she placed them. "This cake will have five layers?"

"Yes. Great job. When I cut, I have to make sure the knife is straight up and down." Millie started cutting the layers.

"What do you do with the extra?"

"There's a lady finger desert I make with bits and pieces. Seems to go over well."

"Filling's ready," Stella announced. "I'll get the icing while you slice the layers."

Millie used the tool that slid through the layer. She separated the parts and spread lemon filling before putting the parts together again. She put the largest layer on the spinning wheel.

Becky and Lindsey leaned across the counter to watch. "What's that for?" Becky asked.

"Makes it easier to ice the cake. Each layer gets a thin coat of icing and then they'll be draped in fondant."

The girls watched with rapt attention as Millie swirled the cake in buttercream icing. Stella then brought the fondant. Three layers would be silver, and two layers would be burgundy.

Lindsey gaped. "You can eat that? It's too pretty."

Millie cut the extra fondant. "Want to try some?" Each of the girls took a small wedge. Their looks of rapture made Millie and Stella laugh. "I think they like it."

Stella's phone buzzed, and she glanced at a text. "Hugh wants me to run an errand with him. He says Aunt Lettie gets to go home today." She looked at Millie. "I'll meet you at the pizza parlor?"

Millie nodded. "Invite Hugh. We'll get these cake layers put up and then the girls can box their cookies for the run."

By the time they got close to five, the thought of pizza made clean-up difficult. Millie shewed them from the kitchen. "Get your coats. I can clean this later."

Becky and Lindsey didn't need convincing.

"Don't forget my bag," Lindsey said, pointing at the pink package tied with ribbons.

"I got it," Millie assured.

A horn honked, and the girls ran through the back door. Millie sighed. Bowls, dishes, flour across the counter, pans in the sink—there would be a ton of clean up. Thinking about the girls' smiles as they boxed cookies for the event would be worth the late night.

She locked the back and skipped over to the car. Dane rolled the window down. "Hop in."

Millie peeked. "Where's Sylvia?"

"She'll meet us there."

Millie went around to the passenger side.

"I smell cookies. Where's mine?" Dane used the rearview mirror to ask the girls.

"These are for Lindsey's parents," Becky raised the pink package. "You'll have to go in and buy yours like everyone else."

"Ooh, you've been told," Millie teased. "You better hope there are cookies left in the window when you go to work Tuesday."

He grinned. "I know a baker, I bet I can get her to help."

"I don't know, I hear bakers are pretty stingy about giving goods away."

"And you can't blame her," Becky added from behind them. "She's worth it."

"I'm beginning to realize that."

His glance made Millie warm, and she looked out the darkening window. "I'll be glad when spring gets here, and we have more daylight."

"I have special lamps set up around my room. Did you know there are light bulbs that can simulate sunshine?" Lindsey responded.

"Can you tell a difference?" Millie scooted in her seat to better see the girls.

Lindsey nodded. "I close my eyes and imagine laying in a sunflower field."

"That would be beautiful."

"Sometimes it's a tulip field. I told my parents I want to visit Holland when the tulips bloom. I think we're going next year."

"I imagine they can't wait to fulfill that dream for you."

"I told them they didn't have to, but I think they're more excited about it than I am."

Millie looked at Dane. He knew. Their excitement wasn't so much about going as it was going with their daughter.

"Here we are," Dane announced as he pulled into an empty parking slot near the front door of the pizza parlor.

"Over here. I nabbed a table already."

A woman with curly blond hair waved as she hollered across the pizza parlor. Becky and Lindsey ran ahead. Dane put his hand on her back and leaned closer. "Sylvia's my older sister, in case you were wondering. I'm pretty sure I learned any bad habits from her."

"Great. This should be interesting."

Sylvia moved in for a quick hug. "You're the troublemaker. I'm glad to meet you."

Becky stood next to her mother. "Miss Millie didn't cause any trouble. Her cookies are good. I'm going to make you a batch when we get home tonight."

Sylvia hugged her daughter. "Baking cookies can wait until after school tomorrow. Come on, let's have a seat."

They piled around the table. The waitress tugged on an empty chair, but Millie held on to the seat. "My sister'll be here in a minute." She checked the message on her phone. "Yes, she's parking now, with Hugh." She looked at the waitress. "We'll need one more seat."

"What do you want to drink?" a nondescript waitress asked with her pencil hovering above a spiral notepad. They went around the table. The waitress left without any further comments.

"No." Dane frowned at Sylvia. "Don't even think it."

"Afraid of the competition?"

Millie glanced back and forth between the two.

Dane shook his head. "The goal has been, and notice I stress been, as in past tense. The goal has been to get the waitress to engage with us. She's already heard about us and knows better than to say anything."

Becky rolled her eyes. "Mom, you're goofy."

Lindsey nudged Becky. "Yeah, but she's good at getting people to chat."

"We'll see about that." Dane sat straighter and pulled his sleeves up.

Millie saw Stella and Hugh and waved them over. "This is my sister, Stella, and an old high school friend, Hugh." She introduced them around the table.

"Those glasses are cool," Lindsey exclaimed.

Stella smiled as she took the empty seat beside Millie. "I love your hat. That's a great color for you."

"Couple more weeks, I won't need it anymore."

The waitress placed a glass of water in front of Lindsey. "Did you have chemo? Was it scary? My little brother is starting in the new year."

Lindsey nodded. "It was rough." She grabbed Becky's hand. "But I have terrific friends who stayed with me. Makes a huge difference."

The waitress finished putting the drinks around without conversing with anyone else. She stared at Stella until Stella pointed at Millie's soda. Hugh opened his mouth to make a selection, but the woman walked away. Millie chewed on her lip to keep from laughing.

Dane lifted his glass. "Kudos to Lindsey. She wins this round. What does everyone want on their pizza?"

Hugh chuckled. "Someone better order for me or I won't get anything."

A variety of options were hollered around the table. They settled on three pies, one veggie, one plain, and one half the works and half pepperoni.

Sylvia nudged Millie. "I looked at that letter. It seems to indicate there's a clause in the lease regarding fines."

Stella looked around. "Letter? What letter?"

"That lawyer sent a letter. At least, I think it's his company. I found it at home yesterday."

Stella frowned. "Why didn't you tell me?"

"I wanted to hear what a lawyer thought about it first."

Stella opened her mouth, then closed it as she breathed a few times through her nose. She kept her voice quiet. "Why wouldn't you show it to me first? We're partners."

"You were going to meet Hugh."

"It wasn't a date, we were talking."

"I'm sorry," Millie blinked against the unexpected sting in her eyes. She and Stella rarely disagreed on anything. Why hadn't she told her about it first? "I should have told you."

"There will be more to tell if I can look at your lease." Sylvia offered.

"What is the letter about?" Stella asked.

"The property owner is taking steps to negate the lease."

Stella grabbed hold of Millie's arm. "Negate, as in break our lease? Why?"

"I would need to see the lease to know for sure."

"Of course," she looked to Millie. "It's okay, right?"

"Yes. I apologize for not telling you yesterday."

"Don't let it happen again."

Becky studied them. "Are you done fighting?"

Stella laughed. "We're sisters. We never stop fighting. Do you have a sister?"

She shook her head. "I keep telling mom and dad, it isn't too late."

Sylvia rolled her eyes. "It is definitely too late."

"There are advantages to being an only child," Stella and Millie offered.

"Especially with a sister like mine." Dane frowned.

Sylvia grinned. "Hey, I was the only child for several years. You're the one who spoiled it."

"You know I like a challenge."

Stella groaned. "No more challenges. Do you know what these two been up to since Thanksgiving?" Stella pointed at Millie and Dane.

Sylvia nodded. "I heard. He tried to get me to help paint."

"I managed on my own with no one the wiser."

"Until you came into the bakery with a splotch of yellow on your shirt sleeve."

Dane shook his head. "Did not."

"I saw it when you handed over your money. That's how I knew for sure it was you."

"Isn't graffiti bad?" Becky looked confused. "Did you get in trouble?"

Hugh grunted. "I think there was plenty of trouble."

Sylvia nodded to her daughter. "Yes, graffiti is bad. Grownups should behave like adults, not do silly pranks."

"If you say so." Dane humored his sister even though he winked at Becky. He turned to Millie. "But I'm not sure what set it off."

"What do you mean, not sure? You put a sign on the sidewalk that said fresh-baked cookies and cocoa."

"But that was my fault." Becky's eyes opened wider.

Millie smiled at her. "I know that now. You have a great reason for what you're doing." She jerked her head toward Dane. "I kind of like bothering your uncle, though."

"Be careful. He'll get you in trouble."

"I know, right?"

Hugh leaned back in his seat. "This is the best entertainment I've witnessed in ages."

Millie laughed. "This from a city slicker?"

He held up his hands. "I grew up in the country."

Stella grinned, looking at Becky and Lindsey. "That was a *long* time ago."

Millie nodded. "Doesn't even have a decent coat for winter."

"Wow." Dane shook his head. "These sisters like to harp on anyone, huh?"

"Pizza's here," Millie slapped his arm. "Let's get it while it's hot."

Hugh looked around, then spoke in a loud voice. "I still don't have a drink."

Stella giggled, then offered him the cup of water that came with her soda.

After a word of thanksgiving, the table quieted as people enjoyed their slices.

Becky eyed the final slice of pepperoni. "May I?"

Dane groaned. "I couldn't eat another bite. You girls'll have to finish the rest of it." He wagged his finger at Becky and Lindsey.

They giggled. "There's too much for us. We'd explode." Becky demonstrated until her mother shut her down with a look.

"If we're all done, I think we better call it a day. Got to get this one home to her parents." Sylvia pointed her thumb at Lindsey.

Stella pushed her seat back. "I'd suggest a walk around the block, but its freezing outside."

"Makes the coming of spring all the sweeter."

Sylvia stood, and Becky and Lindsey followed her.

"I'll see you at home," Stella said as she stood. Hugh jumped up to help her with her coat.

"I rode with Dane and the girls. I've got to go back and get my car."

"I'll take you," Dane interjected before Stella could offer.

"Stella can take me. You don't have to worry about it."

"It's not a problem. I'm heading that direction anyway."

Stella smiled. "Great. I'll see you at home." She took off before Millie could convince her otherwise.

"Looks like it's you and me, kid." Dane dropped a tip on the table.

"Fine." But Millie shrugged into her coat faster than he could offer to help.

The ride back didn't take long. Millie let the Christmas music playing on the radio fill the silence between them. Dane moved his car toward hers, but she stopped him. "I need to run inside. Thanks for the ride and joining us for dinner. I had fun."

"Still looking forward to our concert coming up Friday?"

"Yes, I am." Millie hurried from the car to the back door of the bakery. She waved at Dane, then scrambled to get out of the cold. Lights were still on inside the bakery, and the mess looked worse than what she remembered. She was tired and didn't want to stay. "Should have told Stella you needed a hand," she muttered to herself. She moved dishes that needed to be washed to the sink area. The water took a minute to heat before she could wet a towel to wipe down the equipment. Someone banged on the back door as she wiped the motor compartment of the mixer.

She didn't unlock it, but yelled, "what?"

"It's Dane. Everything okay?"

She recognized his muffled voice and opened the door to let him in. "I'm fine. Cleaning up. We didn't get time to do it earlier."

"I thought you were coming in for a moment. I waited."

"That was sweet of you, but, as you can see," she swept her hand through the air, "I'll need another minute."

"I'll help."

"Not necessary," she tried to protest.

"It was my idea that helped make the mess. Least I can do is help you clean it up."

She took a moment, and then nodded. "You're right, it was your idea. Start washing dishes."

He put his hand to his forehead. "Yes, ma'am."

With Dane's help, they managed to finish the clean-up in less than an hour. Millie fixed a cup of hot chocolate for them both.

"What about the marshmallows?" Dane asked as she handed him a cup.

"Right here." She pulled two large marshmallows, placing one in his drink and one in hers.

They sat at a bistro table near the front door. "Look, it's starting to snow," Dane pointed at the large flakes falling. The backlight of streetlamps made them easy to see.

"It's beautiful. I know winter seems long, but I love to watch falling snow."

"Is that why you've always lived here?"

"College wasn't here, but there's no other place I'd want to be. How did you end up in St. Ives?"

"My sister. I needed change. She told me all about this charming town. I've wanted to open a rare and used bookstore since I was a teenager. I had boxes of books stacked in the garage. One of many things my wife hated."

"That's too bad. And it's a charming shop, even if the name isn't original."

"What do you mean? Book Shop is the original name of the bookstore."

"Not original as in not unique or clever."

"I get it, but there's no use being jealous. Brilliancy is a gift and talent, not available to any old person."

"Calling me old?" She laughed as she tried to push him from his chair.

He jerked her forward, and she squealed as the back legs came up off the floor. He held her, making sure she wouldn't fall. Then one of them moved, and he was kissing her.

When they came up for air, Millie sighed.

"Chocolate's going to get cold."

"Is that a bad thing?" He was still close enough to feel his breath across her cheek.

"Yes." She backed up.

He scooted back in his chair. "Alright. We will finish our refreshment. What made you start a bakery?"

"I love to cook. Always been good with the pastries and cakes. Stella was interested, we had a bit of money from our parents. All the right events came together."

"I'm sure it was harder than what you make it sound like. Our neighborhood is fortunate to have you."

"We are all part of a team and I can't imagine the team not being together."

He raised his cup. "To teams being together." They bumped their cups. "Let me know when you hear from Sylvia."

"After I tell Stella."

He laughed. "Yes, please tell Stella or she might disown you."

25

A week from Christmas Eve, Monday started early and busy. Millie had a stack of orders to fill. Their usual offerings were set in the window and display cases. Millie dipped her pinky in the mincemeat mix. The flavor worked. She poured pie filling into the prepared shells.

"Mills, Dane's sister's here," Stella called from the front.

"Be right there," Millie answered, shutting the oven door. Mincemeat pies would take forty minutes to bake. She set the timer and brought it with her to the front.

Stella and Sylvia were at a table. "What did you find out?" Millie asked as she sat in the third chair. Minutes after eight in the morning, a few of the other tables were occupied. Millie kept her voice quiet.

"Your lease does have a clause about fines."

"But we haven't been fined for anything."

"The building owner thinks you have." Sylvia looked at them both. "Or are about to."

"What do we do?"

"Go see Carmichael and find out who is feeding him lies."

"I don't want to wait until after Christmas. We need

to meet soon."

Stella agreed. "I'll call his secretary and see when he's available. It's about an hour to Minneapolis."

Millie groaned. "Add another hour in traffic, more because of the season." She turned to Sylvia. "Thanks for your help."

"Let me know if you need legal assistance."

"We will."

After Sylvia left, Millie and Stella stood in the doorway. They could see both the café and the kitchen. "I don't want to lose this place."

Stella agreed. "It's been perfect for us. We're caught up on cooking for a while. I'll run home and see what I can do to make an appointment with Mr. Carmichael. I'll get back before the lunch rush hits." She grabbed her coat. "Should have stored that information on the computer here."

"We aren't that far." Millie turned away when the bell on the front door jangled. "I'll take care of things until you get back. Don't be long."

Through the bakery window, Dane saw Millie filling the display beside the register. The tray appeared to be holding muffins. The cookies Becky had described in detail on the drive home yesterday sat on a different shelf. Getting cookies was a good excuse to go into the bakery. Becky also wanted to see if Millie'd go ice skating with them.

Others were interested in bags of cookies. Customers ahead of him pointed at different cabinets. The tray of cookies dwindled. He caught Millie sneaking glances at him. When it was his turn, he smiled. "Which are the cookies Becky helped with? My mission is to get a dozen."

Millie pulled a pan from the top shelf. "A dozen will finish them up." She reached for a white bag.

"I'm taking my niece ice skating tomorrow afternoon. Want to join us?"

Her hand paused inside the bag. "I don't ice skate."

Dane frowned. "What do you mean? Ice skating is the national pastime in Minnesota."

Millie shrugged, finishing his order. "It's not something I'm good at. Can't even stay up on roller skates, let alone ice blades."

"Have you tried ice skating? If athletes can do it…"

She raised her brow. "I can't throw a football either."

He grinned. "Football players aren't on the ice. Hockey players are."

"You get the idea." She folded his bag. "I'm meant to have two feet on the ground, not try to slip around on the ice."

"I'll hold your hand. Give you lessons. I have knee and elbow pads you can wear if you're afraid of hurting yourself."

Her lips twitched. "Wouldn't that look attractive?"

"Then come and spend time. You don't have to put skates on."

Millie glanced at the line of customers. "I'll think about it."

Not long, he guessed. "Tomorrow at six."

"You realize I get up at three thirty in the morning?"

"I'll have you home by eight thirty."

"I'll think about it. Right now, let me help the next customer."

"Okay. Add a cheese Danish and we're good."

"I'm back," Stella declared, walking through the swinging kitchen door. "Wow, this place got busy fast."

Millie grabbed a bag, but Dane stopped her. "You can put it on a plate. I'm on break. I'll eat it here."

Dane watched Millie greet people in line, talking with them as Stella worked the register. He bit into his Danish. The layers of dough crumbled, and the cheese filling had a sweet bite. She was talented. And her hair bounced as she walked. His smart phone vibrated before he could pursue that train of thought. He glanced at the text. *Help, swamped.* He popped the rest of the Danish into his mouth, pulled his jacket on, and headed into the cold.

A tour bus in town meant Mainstreet buzzed with shoppers. There weren't children in the play section, but a few grandmothers looked over the shelves. An elderly gentleman with white hair and a thin gray mustache stood in front of one of the rare book displays.

"How was your trip to town?" Dane asked as he stepped beside the other man.

"Uneventful. I do these things for my wife's sake. Not my choice. I was surprised to find St. Ives has a decent bookstore. It's a pity most of these downtown shopping districts lack such places."

"It is a pity. Anything you're looking for?"

The man turned to Dane. "You work here?"

He held out his hand. "Baxter Dane. This is my shop."

They shook hands. "Well done, son. I see you have a copy of Hobbit."

"First edition." He nodded.

"How much?"

Dane gave the price and watched the old man's eyes widen. He cleared his throat. "How can you ask that much?"

"I know what it's worth."

"We were stationed in England after the war. I still have my original copy."

Dane whistled. "I hope you care for it like the treasure it is."

"I had no idea it could be worth that much."

"I can help you get any of your books appraised, if you want to know their value."

"I may take you up on that."

Dane handed him a card with the store information. "Give me a call or send an email." The older man wandered away after tucking Dane's card in his pocket. Dane touched the glass. It was a reasonable price for the book, but he still hoped it wouldn't sell. He moved through the shop, talking with browsers to help them find a specific section to focus on. A yap brought his attention to Luna. "Hey, girl." He scratched her ears.

"She's well-behaved, but are you sure a bookstore is a good choice for a dog?"

Dane turned. "Hello, Nora."

"Christmas is getting away from us. When are we getting together?"

"I don't think that's a good idea."

She laughed. "Of course, it is. How about we drive to Minneapolis to a real restaurant?"

He shook his head. "Nora, I'm interested in someone else."

She put her hand on his arm. "I know. I've been here all these years waiting for you to be ready."

He pulled away. "Ready for what?"

"To recover from Christina's death."

He shoved a hand through his hair. "I didn't need to recover from Christina's death. I mean, her death was tragic, but we were getting divorced. She had another man in her life."

Nora moved her hands. "What about us?"

"There is no us." He frowned. "You were Christina's friend and her death hit you hard."

"It's the baker, isn't it? She got in our way."

"I'm sorry, Nora, if I did something to make you think I would have feelings for you. I didn't mean to. You should try a few of those places in Minneapolis and find a man you're better suited to be with. I kind of figured you'd move to the big city. Seems more like your style."

Nora looked around the bookstore. "I never could understand why you didn't prefer a sleek metal shelving system."

"That would be your city-girl senses."

"I thought you and I would head to the city together. Christina wanted to," Nora pouted.

"I bought a shop on Mainstreet." Dane spoke slower.

Nora shook her head. "Now you want to get involved with another shop owner." She sighed. "I'm disappointed, but not surprised." She hugged him, trying to get closer than necessary.

Dane backed away. "Take care." He stepped over the gate into Luna's section of the store and crouched beside the dog, watching Nora stomp out of the shop. "That was weird." He scratched Luna's ears as the dog tried to lick his cheek. Her tail thumped the floor. "Don't tell Millie about anything."

"Tell me what?"

Dane jumped to his feet, turning toward Millie. "When'd you get here?"

She tilted her head. "I just arrived to run Luna in the parking area out back."

"Nora was here. I think she may consider moving to the city."

"I don't understand why she came back after college."

"That's easy. Here, she's a big fish in a little pond."

Millie agreed. "In a big city, she'll either become a shark or get swallowed up by one."

"I hope she can find a nice man in an expensive suit."

"She seems to like your manner of dressing."

"Doesn't matter." He grinned slowly. "My interest lies closer to home. Or work, as the case may be."

Millie blushed, but her eyes seemed to sparkle. "I'm going to take…" She hooked Luna's collar with the leash and opened the gate. She was a few steps away when she turned back around. "I can't make a trip ice skating tomorrow, there's a wedding I'm helping to cater. Maybe after Christmas? I won't put skates on, but I'll go." She continued to the back.

Dane's smile widened. If he could get her to the rink, he'd find a way to get her on the ice.

26

"No, really. This has to stop." Stella frowned at the tall slender man with brown slacks and a tweed jacket beneath his black coat.

"Excuse me?"

"What can I get you?"

"I'm Miles Allister, inspector." He handed Stella a card.

"Of course, you are. Fourth time in two weeks. A bit much, don't you think?"

"Are you concerned about something?"

She pasted a sweet smile on her face. "Not at all. Where would you like to begin?"

"I'll sit over here for a while and watch."

Angela scooted next to Stella. "What's he doing?"

Stella glared. "Trying to intimidate, no doubt. Well, in the words of Elizabeth Bennett, my courage always rises with every attempt to intimidate me."

"Who's Elizabeth Bennett?"

Stella rolled her eyes and pushed the young woman away. "What do they teach in schools these days?"

Twenty minutes later, Grandma Cooke, Aunt Bea, and Aunt Dahlia were moving up the sidewalk hovering around Aunt Lettie who was rolling a walker in front of her. Stella ran to the door. "What are you doing? Is it safe to be up and around this soon?" She held the front door. Aunt Lettie slid inside. "Watch the threshold."

Aunt Lettie paused long enough to hug Stella. "I have the gaggle of geese looking out for me, not you, too."

Stella grinned as she watched the others.

"Give her room." Aunt Bea scooted a table out of the way before hugging Stella.

"How's my favorite granddaughter?" Grandma Cooke asked as she hugged Stella as well.

"You say that to whichever of us is closest."

Grandma Cooke kissed her cheek. "My favorite will always be the one I see, even when you are together."

"I see the peeps are back together." Stella grinned at the group. "Everyone want coffee this morning?"

"I think we should celebrate with hot chocolate," Aunt Lettie declared.

"You have your orders," Aunt Bea agreed.

Stella pushed through the counter to the barrister machine.

"Who is this gentleman?" Aunt Dahlia asked, standing behind Mr. Allister.

Stella tried not to laugh as he pretended to ignore the woman. "He's with the city, Aunt Dahlia."

"I'm sure the city pays enough for you to have a coffee and donut," Dahlia smiled.

Stella watched Inspector Allister sigh before standing up. "Thank you, ma'am, but I already had my breakfast."

Dahlia gazed up at him. Stella recognized the tiny movement of her shoulder and the wisp of a grin. "Oh, great," Stella muttered and turned away. "Angela, four hot chocolates." She peaked across the room. Was that a hint of a smile on Allister's face? "Better make it five." Stella put a variety of donut holes on a plate. "They can share these." Stella took the tray.

"I've worked for the city twenty-five years," Mr. Allister was explaining.

Dahlia smiled. "A man who keeps a commitment. There are too few of you now-a-days, you know."

He stepped out of Stella's way. "I'll leave you to your breakfast."

"Join us, please. I insist." Dahlia pulled out the fifth chair at the table. "We're celebrating Leticia's return."

"What happened?" He took the seat.

"Tripped over my own feet is what happened. I was late for a hair appointment."

"Enjoy, everyone." Stella left the tray in the middle. She didn't dare look at Mr. Allister for fear she'd burst out laughing.

"What is Aunt Dahlia doing?" Angela asked in a quiet voice.

Stella turned her around. "Don't watch them. He may be forced to keep them company for a while, but you can be certain he is still watching us. We have work. Allison should be here by nine. I can help Millie in the back."

Allison showed up early, and Stella pushed into the kitchen. "I think we should call the city and find out how many more inspectors they have."

"Why? What happened?"

"Number four arrived this morning."

"A fourth one? He hasn't been back here."

"The aunts got to him first." Stella grinned. "Take a look."

Millie peeked through the doorway. "The tall man sitting with them?"

"Aunt Dahlia started batting her eyes at him."

"Just what she needs, another conquest."

Stella agreed, but Mr. Allister didn't seem quite as severe now that he had a smile on his face. "I'm going to get our supply order ready. Last push before Christmas."

"Check the preorders. I think we have a pavlova and mincemeat pie in the pile on my desk."

"We can have a delivery on the 28th as well. Do you need anything New Years before that?"

Millie shook her head.

Stella strolled to the dry supply closet with her clipboard. The incorrect order from last week had been fixed. She pulled the ladder and went through the top shelf, double-checking dates.

"That's not a safe way to stand on a ladder."

Stella jumped, grabbing a rung. She turned and glared at Mr. Allister. "It's not safe sneaking up on a person and startling them when they're working."

He didn't bother to reply, and Stella went back to checking inventory.

"If your cold storage is as well-organized as these cupboards, I will have a positive report to write."

"Did Aunt Dahlia get you to try the donuts?"

He adjusted his tie as he searched a lower shelf. "Mrs. Greer is persistent."

"That's one way to look at it."

He cleared his throat, made a mark on his tablet, and pointed behind him. "I'll get my coat and take a look at the refrigerator and freezers."

Stella bit her lip to keep from blurting her thoughts.

Aunt Dahlia had that kind of effect on men. She finished her inventory, making note of what needed to be replenished. She went to the office to check through the preorders and make the list she'd email to Lacie Montgomery. About an hour had passed when she returned to the café. The Widow Peeps were getting ready to leave. Stella hugged Aunt Lettie, who seemed paler than when she'd come in. "I'm glad I got to see you up and about this morning. The girls are taking you home to rest, right? Will Hugh be there to help?"

Aunt Lettie patted Stella's cheek. "There isn't enough room in my house for everyone who wants to hover. But I think you're right. Rest is in order."

"We'll have you home in a jiffy, my dear." Aunt Bea promised. The four of them hobbled out.

Aunt Dahlia winked at Stella. "I gave that nice Mr. Allister my phone number."

Nice? Stella grinned. "I think hanging out with you would do him a world of good. I hope he calls."

The café busied. Stella split her time between helping the front counter and decorating gingerbread men in the kitchen.

"I can't believe they had Grandmom out here this morning." Hugh burst into the kitchen. He saw Stella and made a beeline to the island. "Not only is it freezing outside, she hasn't recovered enough for this much activity. The rehab center agreed to send her home before Christmas, and I agreed to help. I'll send her back if her peeps don't let her rest."

Stella pointed at Hugh with a pastry bag of green icing. "Breathe. You know Aunt Lettie isn't going to do anything she doesn't feel ready to do."

"Her friends can talk her out of being sensible."

"Even the doctor said she was okay to go home, didn't he? With or without your help."

"He told her not to overdo it." Hugh pulled out a stool and sat, picking up a plain gingerbread man and biting its arm off.

Stella frowned at him.

"It's okay, isn't it?" He took another bite of the other arm.

Stella understood his stress. She returned to decorating the series in front of her. "They were here for about an hour and were taking her straight home.

"She could slip and fall. Do they know what that would do?"

"I'm pretty sure the three of them had invisible leashes hooked on her. They were not about to let her step on snow, let alone ice."

The stiff hold of his shoulders relaxed. "It's hard to see her this fragile."

"It's hard to admit they're getting old. Aunt Bea isn't mom's sister, she's Grandma Cooke's sister."

"I can't imagine losing her. Not any of them."

"Lord willing, there are still a number of good years ahead." She switched to a different color icing. "What got us on this morbid topic?"

"Concern for my Grandmother."

"How about you let me know how she's doing tonight, and I'll talk with Aunt Bea. They would never do anything to put her in harm's way."

"Thank you for the cookie. What are you doing tonight?"

"Falling into bed exhausted so we can start this all over again tomorrow."

"Come up to the mansion Sunday? We still have to

wrap those presents."

Stella bent her head to look at him over the top of her glasses. "You haven't taken care of that already?"

He grinned. "What fun is there in wrapping alone? I'll bring brunch."

"Our church has a Christmas special. You could join us for that, and then we can head over afterwards."

"We have a plan." He reached for a decorated cookie, but Stella grabbed a wooden spoon laying on the counter and thwacked his hand. "Ow." He frowned as he shook his hand. "Just say no next time."

She grinned. "But this was more fun. You can have a plain one. I have a few extra."

He grabbed two and took off for the door.

"Hey," Stella called, laughter tinging her voice.

He offered a grin. "At least you aren't throwing things at me." He pushed into the café.

"I'm tempted," Stella hollered after him.

"What are you tempted about?" Millie entered the kitchen through the back door as Stella yelled.

Stella tried to control her smile. "Nothing."

"Was that Hugh I saw?"

Stella's smile widened. "Did you have a good time with Dane?"

"I was walking Luna through a snow drift."

"Did she walk or try to jump?"

"Bounded. And it was cold. I'm looking forward to working near the ovens for a bit. How are things up front? Any more inspectors?"

27

Tuesday afternoon, Stella called Millie to the office in the back of the bakery. "I just got off the phone. Friday is our best chance before Christmas. The secretary said we can meet with Mr. Carmichael." Stella held the note.

Millie hesitated. What about her first date with Dane?

"Allison and Angela will be here. Aunt Bea and Aunt Dahlia will help."

"Yes, I know. It's just..." Millie looked at a splotch on her sneaker, then smiled at her sister. "It's nothing. The appointment's for early afternoon, right? We'll be back in plenty of time. There's that concert. Dane invited me to go with him."

Stella shrugged. "Carmichael's secretary said one. I can't imagine the meeting taking longer than an hour. We'll be back on our way to St. Ives before three."

"Should we take a tin of cookies? Remind him what we're doing here?"

They both smiled. Stella nodded, "Wouldn't hurt."

Adam Carmichael lived old money. The stately office building in downtown Minnesota had been there sixty years. The wood wainscoting in the elevator gleamed, and there were no prints on the mirrored glass. Millie squelched the urge to put a handprint on the mirror. Even the tiled floor gleamed. "A cleaner must come in and polish the floor after every use."

"Hush," Stella whispered.

The elevator opened on the top floor. The secretary greeted them. "Good afternoon. I'm Danielle, Mr. Carmichael's secretary. He's expecting you. Would you prefer water or lemonade?"

Both sisters chose water. Rather than the office they'd been to, Danielle led them to a small conference room. The slightly older woman seemed surprised to see another person in the room, but Millie recognized him. Crossing her arms, she took a step closer. "JT. I forget, are you on the Beane or Reynold's side?"

Danielle checked the pad of paper she held in her hand. "You aren't supposed to be in here."

"What are they doing here?" JT asked with a scowl.

Stella stood tall. "We came to speak with Mr. Carmichael. At least now we know who has his ear."

Millie shook her head. "What is your deal? Why are you trying to close down the bakery?"

"It's a bakery. That prime spot should have something more substantial."

"You're trying to get us out of the location on purpose?"

"Mills, he's not the one we need to speak with," Stella cautioned.

"But I am curious to hear more," Mr. Carmichael came in behind them.

Stella and Millie turned around.

"Ladies, good to see you, although I am sorry this had to happen."

Millie shook hands with Carmichael. "That's why we're here. We don't understand terminating the lease."

"Those fines add up. A lien can be put on the establishment. I don't want my building at risk."

"What fines? We haven't earned any fines."

Mr. Carmichael turned to JT. "Where are your copies?"

"Of what?" Millie asked as she stepped up to the conference table. "We've received no fines, even with four inspectors."

JT pushed a letter toward Mr. Carmichael. He looked at it and then handed it to Millie. "What do you say to that?"

Millie accepted the paper. Stella looked over her shoulder. "We should have brought Sylvia with us," she muttered.

Although the document looked official, it had to be a fake. Millie tapped the contact information. "I would have received a notice. We should call this number."

"Look at the date," Stella pointed. "Isn't that the day Mrs. Grayer visited?"

Millie pulled her smartphone from her purse to check the date. "She's one of the inspectors. She'll vouch for us, there were no legitimate code violations."

Mr. Carmichael invited them to sit. Danielle set a glass of ice water on a ceramic coaster of poinsettias in front of them. Mr. Carmichael waited until his secretary left before continuing. "You're claiming this isn't valid?"

"Not in the least." Stella stared at JT. "You've been after us for a while. Why?"

JT gathered his papers without saying anything.

"You tried to force Aunt Lettie to sign papers after

Hugh refused to cooperate with you."

"I think you should explain yourself, son," Mr. Carmichael waved the document. "If this is false, you could face serious charges."

"Is someone interested in the building?" Millie asked Mr. Carmichael, suspicions growing in her mind.

He nodded. "A start-up restaurant."

She looked at JT. "A restaurant you have a vested interest in, perhaps?"

He sighed, shoulders drooping. "My brother-in-law, and yes, I've invested seed money with him. He got a tour of the building a few years back before the bakery. He didn't have the means at the time to make it happen. He keeps raving about how it's a perfect prospect for the restaurant."

"You risk your law license to get us kicked out?"

"I've done research. St. Ives is a perfect location for fine dining. A diner, a mom and pop place, and a bakery? With the traffic that goes through the town, a better option is needed. This venture is with my sister's husband. Family, you know?" JT crossed his arms over his chest.

"Mr. Reynolds, I suggest you leave. I also suggest you destroy any false documents you've created for this fiasco. I will hold on to this one in case it becomes necessary to reveal your misdeeds. Ladies, are you satisfied if he no longer bothers you or the bakery?"

"As long as we don't see him or any more inspectors for the next six months, we're good."

JT stood. "I've been over-zealous having my personal finances tied up with Beau. None of this has been based on good ideas."

"My firm doesn't use Reynolds and Beane. I've no

need to speak to your superiors. Learn from this bit of grace."

JT left without responding.

Mr. Carmichael turned to them. "I apologize. My in-house counsel is responsible for fact-checking. Didn't occur to me to have this checked."

Millie held her breath. "Does this mean you won't be terminating our lease?"

He smiled. "I see no reason to. You may shred the documents when you get home."

Stella reached for his hand. "Thank you, we appreciate your help."

He handed a card to Millie. "I'm having a Christmas Eve party. Be my guests. Bring dates with you if you like."

"That might be nice," Millie assured as she glanced at the glossy invitation with gold-embossed lettering. "We should get back, we've a bakery to run."

Stella shook his hand again. "We'll see you on the twenty-fourth." She handed the tin to him. "We thought your office could enjoy these."

"Buttering me up, so to speak?" He smiled, a twinkle in his eyes.

"Would you like more for your party on Monday?" Stella asked.

He grinned, putting his hand to his chest. "For myself. Don't want to make the caterers jealous."

He ushered them to the elevator.

"Merry Christmas," Millie waved at Danielle.

Millie and Stella hugged each other with relief when the elevator doors swung shut.

Once outside, the air was frigid, but the sky clear as they headed for their car parked on the street a block over. "I can't believe that little weasel tried to shut down our bakery," Stella huffed, sending billows of white fog from her mouth.

"At least he didn't release rats or worse inside the building."

"Ick. Will you invite Dane to go with you to the Christmas Eve party?"

"Possibly." She wrapped her arms around herself. "Maybe. What about you and Hugh?"

Stella scoffed. "There is no me and Hugh."

"There isn't? You've had a couple of meals together."

"It's been nice to catch up, but there's no going back to high school."

"Thank goodness for that. You're both older and wiser. You can make better choices."

"My choice is not Hugh." Stella beeped the car fob.

Millie let the discussion go as they got in the car, but there did seem to be a bit too much protest going on.

28

Dane checked his watch and then his phone. Where was Millie? Dinner reservations would be lost in ten minutes. The bakery was dark. That was no help. Luna hadn't come to the shop today. He paced across the hall. Why hadn't he gotten her number yet? He should drive to the house. But what if she showed up here?

Lights from a car moved along the back wall. Dane jumped up to check the front. Whoever it had been kept going. He looked up the street. Bakery still dark.

"I'll go by the house," he muttered. He paced back to the office, took time to make a sticky note with his phone number to put on the back door. With that done, he turned the last of the lights off, slammed the door, and locked it.

Lights were on at the house, but neither sister were there. Luna barked from inside. He should have brought the sticky notes to leave a message on her door. Of course, she could have called the shop if she didn't have his number. Dinner was a bust. He looked at his watch. No reason to go to the concert.

"Can't say I didn't try to find you," he saluted the house, then checked the street. No one was coming. It was too cold to sit around and wait. He might as well head home.

"I hate city traffic," Millie whined again as she shook her phone.

"No service yet?"

"No, and the battery's about dead."

"He'll understand."

"Or he'll never speak to me again. This'll be like one of my pranks."

"We'll be home in less than an hour. What time was dinner?"

"Six. The concert starts at eight."

"We'll get you home and you'll call him. Maybe pick up a slice of pizza. You can still enjoy the concert together."

"When did you become such a romantic?"

"Romance is sweet when I'm not the one involved."

"How would you know? You haven't dated anyone seriously in the past ten years."

"Look who's talking."

Millie sighed. "We best do something about it or end up old maids with a house of cats."

"I'd prefer dogs. Just saying. Besides, Dane might be the real thing."

"If he talks to me after tonight. Oh no, it's dead." Her screen blanked. Millie checked the glove compartment once more for the car power charger. "Are you sure it isn't here?"

"Not unless it magically appears. Look, home sweet home."

Millie ran from the car before Stella came to a complete stop. "Will you take care of Luna? Poor baby's been in the bathroom all day."

"I've got her, get going."

Millie took a few precious minutes to change into a black dress with a skirt that poofed out. Hose and shoes with a wide heal rounded out the outfit. She added a red scarf, dragged a brush through her hair, and applied lipstick and a bit of eye color. Once ready, she used the computer to get the shop's phone number. With her phone plugged to the wall, she was able to place a call.

"I'm sorry. We had to run to Minneapolis this afternoon. I thought I'd be back in plenty of time, but traffic turned into a nightmare and I'm sure you know how dead reception gets between here and the city." She gasped for breath. "We needed to use my phone to find the place and it died by the time we got home. I'll run by the store first. If nothing else, I'll meet you at the concert. Please be there. I promise I'm sorry and I didn't do this on purpose."

Millie checked the power. Still wasn't enough to take it with her. She ran to Stella who was serving Luna dinner. "Do we have a charger in the house that'll work in the car?"

"I don't think so."

"I'm going to run by the book shop. If he isn't there, I'll go to the concert. If he calls the house or comes by here, tell him to meet at the concert."

"I got it. Get going. I can't wait to see how this turns out."

"You and me both, sister."

Millie drove down Mainstreet. The front of the bookstore had the single light over the book tree. Everything else was dark. He could be in the office. She drove around to the back.

She stopped the car by the back door and then got

out. "Can't believe I forgot my coat." Cold bombarded her as she clomped to the door in her thick heals. She banged and waited. There didn't seem to be any action. She checked the parking lot, but his vehicle wasn't there. "Okay, concert hall." She shivered as she flopped into the car. She turned the heat to high.

The concert hall was a crowning achievement for St. Ives. The lot was packed. There were also four possible points of entry. Why hadn't she brought her phone? She managed to find a parking space wedged between two pickups, although it seemed like three blocks away. She looked in the back of her car, but there was no coat or extra wrap. "I am adding an emergency coat to this car."

She got out and started to walk. Her fingers and toes were numb by the time she reached the first entry. "I'm looking for Dane." Could he understand her through chattering teeth? "Um, Baxter Dane. Has he shown up?"

The usher checked his list on the clipboard. "Nah, not through this entry. You'll have to go around front."

"Can I cut through inside?"

He shook his head. With a silent groan, she continued. The next usher was a plump middle-aged woman who took more notice of her predicament.

"Honey, you are frozen. What are you doing without your coat? Get in here."

She brought her into the bright, blessedly warm foyer. "Thank you. Has Baxter Dane checked in? I'm supposed to meet him."

She checked her list and shook her head.

Millie sighed. "Do I have to walk around to the next entrance?"

"I've got a radio, dear. Let me check and see." She pushed a button. "Otis, do you have a Baxter Dane on your list? You do? Is he here? Is he waiting on a young lady?"

There was a buzz of static, and then a reply. "He's already with a woman. His original didn't show up and he didn't want the tickets to go to waste."

"Well, thank you Otis." She pressed the walkie talkie to her chest. "That's too bad, hon. And we're sold out tonight."

"I know." Millie gulped. He gave her ticket to another woman? Had he brought Nora? He brought Nora, didn't he?

The walk back to the car was even more miserable. Cold air bit her nose and made her eyes water. There was no other reason for moist cheeks. She wrapped the scarf around her arms as best she could. Her legs ached with cold. Her hands were shaking hard by the time she reached her car. Keys slipped through her fingers twice.

"Good heavens, what are you doing? You'll catch pneumonia."

Millie managed to turn. "Dane?"

"Yes. I got your message." He pulled his coat off and wrapped it around her. "I've been driving up and down the aisles looking for your car."

"They said you were inside with Nora." She managed to chatter.

He rubbed her arms. "Come on, my car's still warm."

He wrapped his arm around her shoulders, and she didn't stumble. He set her in the passenger seat. Even with his coat and out of the wind, she was trembling all over. He started the car. He turned, taking her hands in his. "Good grief woman. You're frozen."

"I am officially a popsicle."

"Why? You've lived here all your life. You know how dangerous these cold temperatures can be."

Her feet were starting to tingle. Thawing out would be a painful process. "I didn't realize I'd have to walk half a mile to get to the building. Then the guy on this side wouldn't let me in. I had to walk around the front." Her teeth chattered. "I sound like a telegraph machine."

He wrapped her hands in his, then held them close to his mouth, blowing on them.

"Who did you give the tickets to?"

"My sister."

"Not Nora?"

"No, not Nora." He laughed. "When will you get that through your thick skull?"

"I know." Most of the shaking had passed, although shivers course through as her legs complained. "Just making sure. It's what we women do."

"Your color looks more normal. Starting to feel better?"

"Much. Except I ruined our first official date. Minneapolis took longer than expected and circumstances stacked against us."

"It's one date. I'm not plotting the rest of my life on its failure. Speaking of which, where's your phone?"

"At home. It died, and Stella's car charger disappeared."

"Of course, it did. When we get to your house, I'm putting my number in your phone. Here." He handed her his phone. "Are your fingers working again?"

She wiggled them.

"Good. Add yourself to my contacts."

"Positive?"

"Absolutely."

"Absolutely positive?"

"Yes," he growled. "Why are you smiling like that?"

"It's what my sister and I do, although she doesn't growl at me."

"At least I didn't roar."

She put her name and number in his phone. "I think I'm ready to go back to my car."

"I'll follow you home."

"Yes, dad."

"I'm not being dad-protective."

"Then what would you call it?"

"Man falling in love."

The confession was unexpected. Millie opened her mouth, but had he said what she thought she heard?

"Stunned silence isn't always the best sign."

"Ice-addled brain," she said as she tapped her head.

He leaned closer. "How do you feel about love."

"I like love. Love is special." His eyes had flecks of green. She was trying not to look at his lips, but they were warm and inviting. "Um," whatever she meant to say was lost when he kissed her.

Practice was doing them good. His hands were in her hair and butterflies were diving like crazy in her stomach as their kiss deepened. He pulled away, but his hands toyed with her ears.

"Yeah, I think I'm falling fast." His voice made her legs go weak.

"I'll be right there with you."

"That's almost as good as telling me you care."

"You're not getting your coat back until we get to

my house."

"Nice transition." He pulled something from his pocket. "Here are your keys."

Things to say whirled through her head, but she didn't know where to start.

He pressed a quick kiss to her lips. "We'll talk when we get to your house. Stella won't mind if I come in, will she?"

Millie shook her head. He was close, and she slipped him a kiss.

He kissed her back. "We aren't a couple of teens alone in the car for the first time."

She giggled. "You may need to push me out, it's cold out there."

"We can always come back for your car tomorrow."

"No. I'll be heading to the bakery before the sun's up."

"Then get, so we can head for the house." He leaned past her and pushed the door open.

Cold blasted into the warm car. Millie grabbed her keys and got out. Even with the short distance, she was shivering by the time she unlocked the car and got in. Cold air through the vents didn't help. She pushed the dial to full heat. The coat smelled like Dane. She pushed her nose into the collar. He smelled good, woodsy. She pulled out of the parking spot. He said he was falling in love with her? Did she feel the same? "I've never noticed anyone the way I notice him. Even when I thought I didn't like him, I noticed whenever he was near." Great. Now she was talking to herself. She switched on the radio and headed for home.

29

"Where did they come from? Did someone drop a dozen buses at the end of Mainstreet?" Allison groaned as she hurried to the counter with the expresso order.

"Any word from Angela?" Stella pressed numbers into the register, took the card, and completed the transaction. Allison shook her head. Stella patted her shoulder as she moved to the next specialty drink. "You're doing great." Stella heard the door to the kitchen open.

"I hope one of the Peeps show up," Millie said. "We need help back here."

The doorbell jangled, and Stella saw a familiar suede jacket. She pushed through the crowd to Hugh.

"Look at you," he said with a smile.

She grabbed his hand. "Perfect timing. Come help." He didn't hesitate, and she led him to the register. "Take orders. Your sister'll fix drinks. You get baked goods. If it's a to-go order, write it on here," she tapped a pad of sticky notes. "Put the note on the kitchen door and knock twice. Be sure to have their name with the order. We'll take care of it."

"I can run a register," he assured her.

"I know you're brilliant." She squeezed his hand and went to help Millie. "Where do you need me?" She asked her sister.

"Did Angela arrive?"

"No, but Hugh came in. I put him on the register."

She nodded. "I want to do a couple dozen stars with blue sprinkles on them."

A few dozen turned into eight. Hugh peeked through the kitchen door. "We've earned a break. The entire Mainstreet is on fire tonight."

"I don't know where they came from, but there will be lots of happy business owners."

Milly accepted a mug of tea. "Better than small business Saturday. Join us, Hugh." Millie motioned to the seat across from Stella. "Where's Allison?"

"She took off when the line of customers dwindled. She had a bag of goodies for Grandmom."

"Thank you for helping out." Stella smiled at him.

"Do I get to keep the tips in the jar?"

She furrowed her brows. "If you insist. We donate tips to a mission's group for orphans."

"Oh, well, yes. Let me have the tips instead. I am much more worthy than a mere orphan." He scoffed but accepted the cookie.

Millie shook her head at the two of them. "You think I'm bad? I'm going to Dane's to get Luna."

"Must be time to head for home." Stella said as they watched Millie wrap up and leave.

"I have a better idea." Hugh stood, holding his hand to Stella.

"What?"

"The bakery might be closing, but the shops are open a few more hours. Sleigh rides. Walking beneath the lights."

"You mean freezing?"

"Cold is part of the Christmas experience. That's what makes hot chocolate good."

"Do you think people in Australia pretend to have a cold Christmas?"

"We should head down under and find out."

"You let me know when you get there."

Hugh pulled her seat back. "Get your coat, scarf, and mittens. Tonight, we'll do Christmas in style."

Stella sighed, but she jumped to her feet. At least she had corduroy pants that slipped inside her blue-stained calf boots. The matching long sleeve T-shirt coordinated with her blue glasses. Hugh held her apricot-colored thigh-length coat that fit at the waist and flared out. She tied the belt as Hugh shrugged into his coat.

"A bit more practical than the suede," Stella complimented.

"I was told I looked dapper." He struck an odd pose.

"Don't do that." Stella grabbed his arm and pulled him to the front door. "Let's go."

The soap store next door didn't hold interest for either of them. They continued to the Russian gift store with a larger than life Saint Nicholas standing beside the front window. "We need a picture with Santa." Stella pulled Hugh beside her as she tried to grab hold of her smartphone.

"A selfie with Father Christmas? What did we do before these magical machines?"

"Use regular digital cameras. My arm's too short. You'll have to hold it."

"Like this?" His first shot had their chins.

"No. Come on, you can do it. Angle up a little."

"But then you get too much nostril."

Stella giggled. "You might have too much, I'm perfect."

"Don't say such things, tragedy will befall us." He raised his arm a little more. "How's this?"

"Smile nice. I want a picture Aunt Bea and Aunt Lettie can enjoy."

"We should look for a pair of frames." He leaned their heads together more and managed a decent shot. "I might want one of these as well."

"You want a picture with just you and Santa?"

"No, a copy of the one with the three of us. Proof we went Christmas shopping."

"Let's look in the shop." Their looking didn't last very long. The owner glared at their giggling exploration of the discount table.

"The bookstore is next," Stella rubbed her hands together since she didn't put her mittens on. "He'll be nicer to us."

Dane and his assistant walked among a few late shoppers as Stella and Hugh entered the shop. "I'm going to stand at the fire for a quick warm up," Stella pointed. Hugh followed her.

"Hey, Stella." Dane greeted. "Millie picked up Luna."

"I know. We decided to go shopping tonight with the stores open late. Did Millie go home already?"

"She was yawning. Figured it must have been a long day."

"And a busy night. Good thing most of our Christmas orders are finished."

Dane shook hands with Hugh. "Good to see you

again. We have hot chocolate and tea over there. Help yourself." He grinned. "You don't have to wait for a waitress."

"Thanks. I like your setup here." Hugh admired an old Dutch buffet. "Can we browse?"

"Sure." Dane moved on to greet a customer entering the bookstore.

Hugh picked up an old WWII can. "I'm used to bookstores having rows after rows of books. I like the way these rooms flow."

"I think he has rare books as well. You should ask if he has anything from the era of your St. Ives mansion."

"Great idea, Einstein. I'll call him after the holidays and make an appointment to discuss it."

They meandered a while, fixed a couple of drinks to carry with them, and burst into the cold again. The next corner over had a short line for a carriage ride. Hugh nudged Stella. "Shall we?"

"If they've got blankets, I'm game."

The wait didn't take long. Hugh pulled himself into the carriage and then offered Stella a hand up. Not only were the blankets wool, there was a heating element through the seat. Stella sighed. "This is bliss. I always wanted heated seats in my car."

"Look." Hugh pointed at the sky. "We're a block from Mainstreet and already the sky looks better."

"So many stars." Stella sighed, leaning against Hugh as she looked up.

Hugh wrapped his arm around her shoulders. "Do you still wish on stars?"

"Wishes?" She shrugged. "I don't need wishes. I have a business I love, working with my sister. There's not much of my life I feel needs to change."

"What about love? Having a special man in your life?"

"If it happens, it might be nice. What about you? You haven't said much about your almost wife."

"I don't feel like talking about her tonight. How about we enjoy tonight and save the serious discussions for later?"

"Agreed." Stella remained where she was with Hugh's arm around her. The carriage turned back toward town and before long they were disembarking and retrieving their now-tepid teas.

The walk through town turned amiable in its silence. Hugh pushed his hands into his coat pockets and rubbed his foot across the sidewalk. Stella felt light inside, almost bubbly, as they stood in front of the bakery.

"I'm glad we are closed for Sunday. Will you meet us at church for advent?"

"Can't make it tomorrow. I will Christmas Eve. At least, I hope I will."

"Do they need you at the mansion?"

He laughed. "The city manager wants to talk. Not sure why it has to be tomorrow, but I told the ladies I'd meet with him and then let them know. I know how much church means to them. Grandma Keyes is planning to attend, even."

"That will be good for her," Stella placed her hand on his arm. 'She broke a little, but she isn't broken."

"She's the only mother I've known. It's scary."

"Millie and I agree with you there. We don't want to see any of them aging. But we can't let our fears interfere with their lives." A cold wind seeped around her scarf. "Brrr. I better go before I turn into a pumpkin.

We'll see you tomorrow at dinner."

"Have fun at church. Don't catch anything on fire."

She made a face, ignoring the memory of Mrs. Waddle's fur coat. Singed hair did not make a pleasant smell.

30

The church of St. Ives had a tall steeple that could be seen from the town center. Millie and Stella waited near the open front doors where the morning sunlight managed to shine, watching as Aunt Bea, Aunt Lettie, Aunt Dahlia, and Grandma Cooke shuffled toward them. All four of the Widow Peeps wore classic hats. Aunt Dahlia had a crimson fedora cap with black netting. Aunt Bea and Grandma Cooke had the same couture hat with a short rim in the back and longer rim in the front. Aunt Bea's was green, and Grandma Cooke's was red. Aunt Lettie's hat was a bowler cloche with a poinsettia curling across the front.

Stella kissed Aunt Bea's cheek once they arrived at the doors. "I thought my vintage dress with these bows and packages would take the cake." Her phone buzzed. She glanced at the text.

Millie laughed. "I'm thankful this skirt is long and keeps my legs warm." She fiddled with the velvety green material, then followed as they entered the church.

Once seated in the pew, Stella leaned over to Millie. "Think you can get a ride home with Aunt Bea? Hugh wants help at the mansion wrapping gifts." She waved her phone with the message.

"Stells to the rescue, huh?" Millie leaned closer to Aunt Bea. "Did the four of you drive together?"

Aunt Dahlia scooted. "I drove myself. You need a ride?"

Millie nodded. "Home for an afternoon would be lovely."

Plans in place, they enjoyed the caroling and listening to the Christmas story. The organ hummed Hark the Herold Angels Sing as the fourth advent candle flickered. Millie leaned into Aunt Bea. This was her favorite part.

Pastor Rhodes took the candle lighter from a child before smiling at the congregation. "Be sure to join us Christmas Eve. The light of the world has come. Let's pray, and we will be dismissed."

Children pushed out from their seats while amen hung in the air. Millie and Stella waited until the aisles cleared. "I'll grab her walker." Stella hurried to the back of the church

Millie squeezed Aunt Bea's hand. "It never gets old."

"Christmas is a very special time of year," Aunt Bea agreed.

"How wonderful we get to spend it with family and dear friends." Grandma Cooke straightened her hat.

"Here we are," Stella sang. The others left the pew so Aunt Lettie could hobble to her walker. She took hold of the handles then lifted each of her legs.

"Are you okay?" Millie asked, her hand on Aunt Lettie's back.

"The pew is not the most comfortable. Just stretching."

"I'm glad you were able to join us."

Grandma Cooke waved at Pastor Rhodes as they passed. "Now we should get her home. A few of those exercises will work out the kinks."

Aunt Lettie grinned at Millie. "Care to join us? Nothing as entertaining as watching three old goats try to be graceful."

Millie laughed. "I have a puppy who's going to show me how graceful I can be chasing her around the yard. I'll see you at dinner." She followed Aunt Dahlia to a red Chrysler LeBaron. At least the top was up.

"I can't wait for spring," Aunt Dahlia patted the soft roof. "Sweet air in your face."

"And tangles in your hair." Millie added with a chuckle.

"Worth the price." Aunt Dahlia promised.

***

Stella checked her face in the rearview mirror before leaving for the mansion. She was smiling. "You should know better." Aunt Dahlia honked as they passed. Stella waved then turned in the opposite direction toward St. Ives.

Hugh wasn't outside, so she walked around to the back and let herself in. From the open kitchen, she could see what appeared to be the butler's pantry. Bags were piled on the table, along with an assortment of wrapping paper, a few bows, and a pile of ribbon that moved. Stella placed her purse on the counter beside the refrigerator as she watched the little pile. A fuzzy tail poked out from one side then disappeared within the tangle. She stepped beside the pile, her red shoe barely touching the ribbon, and wiggled her shoe a little. A silvery paw darted through the melee. "What have we here?" Stella bent and dug into the pile for the warm little body. The kitten didn't mind being pulled out. "Where did you come from?"

"You found her," Hugh gasped, sounding relieved.

Stella held the kitten against her chest. "She's your cat?"

"Not officially. I found her in the stables."

"Do you have food for her? And kitty litter? Store's will be closing early today."

He shook his head. "I've taken care of all that. I brought her over here so she wouldn't disappear, and then she disappeared."

"Hiding in the ribbon. Perfect location, if I don't say so myself." Stella pointed at the bouncing ball for Hugh's niece. "I don't think that's going to wrap too well."

He held up a trash bag. "Brought this. Should be boxes for the purses and wallets. Not sure how you want to handle the kitchen gadgets for Mills."

Stella placed the kitten on the table. "Let's get to it. I'm not missing dinner tonight."

Stella let Hugh do most of the wrapping while she worked on making gift tags from old Christmas cards. "I usually throw my card out by February." She cut and tied a piece of ribbon through the hole she made at the top of the card. The kitten curled up in the box, sleeping. Stella tried not to disturb her as she picked another card.

"This is the last of it." Hugh placed the wrapped box holding Millie's stegosaurus ladle at the top of a pile. "Do you want to take any of these home with you or save them to open at Mrs. Cooke's—I mean Aunt Sylvia's?"

"All ours and the Widow Peeps will go to Grandma Cooke's. When's Stacey coming in with your niece?"

"They'll visit around New Years. I'll keep this pile here until then."

"I'm going to head home and change before dinner." She ruffled her frilled skirt. "I'm still wearing church clothes."

"Well-themed. Can't wait to see what you'll wear on Christmas. Probably won't be the elf costume."

Stella laughed. "Don't remind me. I think I wore that thing two weeks straight in high school."

"You looked adorable, as you know. I don't think anyone minded."

"Wouldn't have mattered." She tapped the card box with a gentle nudge. "Don't forget sleeping beauty here."

"Not a chance."

Stella walked into the kitchen. Reaching for her purse, she turned suddenly. "Did you meet with the city manager this morning?"

"They're having electrical issues in the city hall building. The historical society board approved having the Downtown Christmas Party here. Guess we'll be decorating in the morning."

"That's wonderful news. Much more charming than city hall."

"Mrs. Wright will bring flyers around to the shops tomorrow. Most everyone's open to capture the last drop of Christmas cheer."

Stella wiggled her brows. "We'll have plenty of cheer. See you in a few."

LAURIE BOULDEN

31

By mid-afternoon Monday, the onslaught of Christmas Eve had dwindled to a few last-minute emergencies. The spare pies in the front window display were gone. Angela and Allison fell back onto chairs.

"I don't want to move," Allison groaned.

Millie laughed. "We still have Christmas Eve service and then our party."

"Thought you were going to Mr. Carmichael's gathering?"

"We decided to stay here. Town hall is all the fancy I need."

"It isn't at the town hall," Allison held up a note. "They moved it to Ives Mansion."

"Hugh told me yesterday," Stella said as she perked from her slouch against the counter. "I was so tired with dinner last night, I forgot to mention the news."

Millie stood and stretched. "I'm excited to see it tonight. The kitchen is cleaned up. The front is presentable. We'll take the Christmas decorations down later this week."

"You don't seem worn out," Angela frowned at Millie. "Did you have elves helping in the kitchen?"

"Most of the baking had to be done before today. I'm going to nab Luna and head home. If I don't crash on the couch, I'll meet you at the church." Millie picked up her coat and purse. Once the coat was buttoned, she pulled mittens from the pockets. "Merry Christmas." She hugged Allison. "You, too, Angela" Millie walked through the front into cold. The overcast sky promised snow later. She passed the Russian gift shop and the card store. Dane was in the window straightening the book tree. He saw her and waved. The cold wasn't as bothersome.

"Did you have a crazy day as well?" Millie asked as she closed the door behind her.

"Plenty of typical last-minute frantic shoppers."

Luna heard her voice and barked. Millie glanced down the hallway. "I couldn't get away to walk her earlier."

"I had one of the college kids take her out back." He followed her to Luna's area. "Good to see you're wearing a sensible coat."

"Don't remind me. I don't ever want to feel that cold again."

"Is your phone working?"

"Yes, I think." Millie pulled it from the front pouch of her purse.

Dane took the phone and added himself as a contact.

"Wait," Millie held up her finger as she pressed the camera button. "I'll want a photo to go with that."

He smiled, and then grimaced at the flash. "My eyes, I'm blinded." He covered his eyes with his hand.

She slapped his arm. "Cute."

"Ow. You shouldn't do that, you know. Slap

people. I bet you don't slap your grandmother."

"She's not overly dramatic."

"Me?" He feigned innocence.

"Who'd have thunk it." Millie shook her head. "I had you pegged wrong. Here I thought you were a boring book boy."

"I thought you were a bakery brat."

"Are you going to the Christmas Eve party?"

He looked at his watch. "After the service?"

She nodded. "They've moved the party to the Ives Mansion. Stella says it's worth a gander."

"We won't be able to walk from the church to the Community hall. How about you take Luna home and I'll pick you up."

"I like that plan."

"Will this become official date number one?"

"I'm not sure I want to risk it. We'll go together for convenience sake."

"Whatever makes you happy."

Millie swallowed the urge to tell him he made her happy. She leashed Luna and went out the back to her car.

Dane stood in the doorway and yelled to her, "I'll be there in an hour."

Millie hurried home. Luna danced around her as she took a quick shower and worked curls into her hair once it dried. With her red coat in mind, she picked a black dress that went a little past her knees. Red boots fit over her calves. She pulled the Santa hat from the corner of the mirror and set it on her head. For once, when she glanced at herself in the mirror, she felt as fashionable as Stella.

The doorbell rang. Luna barked. Millie thumped her

way down the steps, getting used to the feel of the boots.

Dane's eyes widened when she opened the door. "Wow. I want a Santa hat."

Millie laughed. "I think I have another."

"Bring it on. Can't be outdone by you." He crouched to play with Luna.

Millie went to the coat closet and grabbed the other Santa hat. "Here," she motioned for him to bend down. She pushed the hat over his silver hair and adjusted the floppy part to fall to the right. "Perfect."

"That you are." He took hold of her hands. "I got you a gift. Do you want it now?"

She stilled, butterflies working overtime. "Should we wait for midnight?"

"Are you planning to stay out that late with me?"

"I can rest most of the day tomorrow, and the next. We're closed the day after Christmas."

"Smart thinking. Wait until midnight. Do you need to put Luna in the bathroom?"

"She's fine. Seems to enjoy sitting in the window waiting for us to come home."

"Where's your coat?"

She handed it to him, and he helped her put it on. Having him close felt good. He took her hand and they walked to the car. Like a gentleman, he got her situated on the passenger side.

***

Stella watched Millie walk past the window, her head bobbing above the painted hills. Dane was good for her, that was clear.

"Hey, I'm out of here," Angela jumped off the counter. She looked at Allison. "Want a ride home?"

"Great." Allison nodded. The girls left.

Stella looked at the shiny postcard used to announce the change in venue. Her phone buzzed in her pocket. "Hello?" she answered without looking.

"I may have bitten off more than I could chew," Hugh sighed. "Think you can come help? Or are you busy at the bakery?"

"We are all cleaned up and I'm the last one out. I can drive over."

"You would be a lifesaver."

"Twizzlers are more my thing."

"Ha. Come around to the front. I'll see you in about thirty minutes."

It took her half that time to get to the estate. "I don't even want to know how fast you were driving," Hugh proclaimed as he opened the door for her.

Stella wore her candy cane glasses and looked at him over the top rim. "You said you needed help."

'Are the glasses prescription or do you wear them for the effect?"

"A woman does not tell her secrets."

"Of course not. How foolish of me to ask."

He tried to hold on to her hand, but she put distance between them. "What help do you need."

"Come see if you approve." He led her through the front this time. "The caterers and workers are the same as were hired for the city hall location. No harping over someone else's sweets."

"This one time, I'll let you get away with it. Wasn't your planning. Which rooms are being used?"

"We'll be in the ballroom. Down here."

She followed Hugh. He led her to a long room on the far side of the castle. She gasped. "This is beautiful." Even with afternoon light streaming through the windows, lights strung across the high ceiling glowed. Christmas trees dressed in gold and silver stood in front of the windows. Tables were set up on one side with an open area for dancing on the other. Even the tables were dressed, covered with red, blue, or white tablecloths and a center wreath with candles.

Stella turned around to face Hugh. "You don't need any help, but you wanted me here anyway. Why?"

"I want to talk."

"We talk all the time."

"Not about what I want to discuss."

"We're friends. After ten long years of silence, we're friends. That's a good place to be."

"I want different."

"Return to Minneapolis. You said yourself there were more and better options."

"I don't want to go back to Minneapolis."

"Then accept things as they are."

"Do you know why I broke my engagement to Dawn?"

"You were good together, but not great."

"It was a card game. Life and death situation, who do you want by your side? Dawn wasn't the first person to pop into my head."

"She must have been hurt."

"Surprised. I think we both were. We'd become comfortable together but splitting up didn't hurt."

"It's good you didn't marry."

"Don't you want to know who came to mind?"

"Your mom."

"No, it was you."

"Ridiculous. We haven't seen each other for ten

years."

"It's the truth. I received the job with the heritage society and was offered a place to stay. Everything lined up for me to return to St. Ives." He took a breath. "And you."

"I'm happy to have seen you."

"There's more to it than that."

She shook her head. "There can't be. Fool me once is on you. Fool me twice is on me."

"Forgive me for being an impetuous college student. I'm not the boy I was then."

"I'm no longer the girl who loved you."

"Then turn around and leave."

She shook her head. "I'm enjoying myself."

"What do you mean, enjoying yourself?"

"Listening to you ask for forgiveness, trying to explain you were too immature for a serious commitment a decade ago." He grabbed her around the waist, and she squealed as she wrapped her arms around his neck. "What are you doing?"

"Trying to figure out if you're going to let me kiss you or not."

She pressed her lips against his cheek. "There. I kissed you."

"That's not my idea of a kiss." He proceeded to show her. Stella didn't mind in the least.

When they pulled apart, he tucked a loose curl behind her ear. "Does this mean you care?"

"No." She rested her hand against his chest. She could feel his heart beating.

"That's sarcasm."

"A natural protective stance when a lot is at stake."

"What's at stake?"

"Us."

He laced his fingers together behind her back. She couldn't pull away. "I am one-hundred percent all in on my side."

"That leaves no room for error."

"I'll make mistakes, without a doubt. But I won't ever stop loving you and wanting what's best for us."

Stella considered for a moment. "I can live with that."

"How do you feel about me?"

"What do you mean?"

"I love you." He waited but she watched him without a reply. "Doesn't me saying I love you make you want to say something back?"

She grinned. "Hold on to your hat, it's going to be a bumpy ride."

He sighed. "I can tell you're going to make it a bumpy ride, aren't you? Wouldn't you prefer a nice smooth sleigh ride in moonlight?"

"Ooh, that is more appealing." She kissed his lips. "I love you. Go find me a sleigh ride."

"I'm in if I find you a sleigh ride?"

"You were in when I jumped over the couch at Thanksgiving, numbskull. A sleigh ride would make for a romantic date." She kissed the end of his nose. "I love you."

He picked her up and twirled her around. Stella held on, laughing. She stopped him. "I need to get ready. I'd rather not wear a Christmas T-shirt and jeans to church."

"I should have had you bring your stuff to get ready here. You could use one of the bathrooms."

"How old are these pipes?" She kissed him.

"I should go with you."

"You can meet me at church."

He grimaced. "I'm meeting the caterers. Don't think I'll be able to make the candlelight service."

She squeezed his hand. "Then I'll see you here, tonight.

He sighed loudly. "Fine."

Stella linked her fingers with his, then stepped back and tilted her head to look at Hugh. He was still watching her. "What?"

"I'm processing."

"Go home and process. Give Grandma Keyes a kiss for me. Tell her I'll see her tomorrow."

The church filled with people. Pastor Rhodes used the Quaker family to light the advent candles. Mr. Quaker lifted his youngest daughter into his arms and helped her reach the Christ candle. He put the lighter on the table and lit a small candle from the flame of the Christ candle. Mrs. Quaker lit her small candle, then they walked to the first-row pew. The overhead lights went out as tiny flames flickered to life through the congregation. Someone started to sing Silent Night. The gentle carol wrapped around them with the soft light. Dane held his candle still as first Millie, then Stella lit their candles.

"Merry Christmas, God bless us everyone." Pastor Rhodes prayed as the hymn ended.

Aunt Bea wrapped an arm around Stella and Millie after candles were extinguished and returned to the box in the foyer. "A candlelight service is a lovely way to begin Christmas."

Ives place looked like a fairytale castle. Trees were draped with white lights. Colors of green and blue were projected onto the stone façade. Santa greeted them at the door. They were led to a ballroom. A DJ set up in one corner had White Christmas playing. A few couples danced. Tables decorated with velvety cloths were on the other side of the room.

Millie removed her coat. "Let's nab a table. Stella should be here, possibly the girls. Did you invite your workers?"

"They seemed more interested in their own plans." He placed her coat across one of the chairs and onto the table. He set his own coat next to hers, and then grabbed her by the hand. "Shall we take a spin around the room?"

"I've never seen you dance."

"I can manage not to step on toes, but I'm never winning prizes."

"I'm a toe smasher," Millie lifted one of her feet, "and I've got boots. Sure you want to risk it?"

"Come on, trouble." He pulled her to the dance space anyway.

As the song ended, Millie waved at Stella across the room. She glanced at Dane. He tilted his head in that direction and Millie weaved her way toward her sister, who stood notably close to Hugh. "You look cozy," Millie smiled at Stella and Hugh.

Stella had changed into a red dress that flared around her knees. She still wore the candy cane glasses, but she had a long red and white Santa cap. Her boots were white. Hugh stood with a hand around her waist. Stella beamed. "He's decided he can't live without me."

"I believe the feeling is mutual."

She grinned. "Details."

Millie smiled at Hugh. "I knew you weren't here for

the house."

"It's an awesome place, but your sister is the real reason I came home."

Dane held out his hand. "Congratulations, although I'm not sure you got the better sister."

Millie joked with her sister, "Go dance before the boys get into something irritating."

Dane nodded. "It's not a bad dance space."

Stella's brows rose. "You danced? With Millie?"

Dane nodded.

Stella scoffed. "Can you still feel your toes?"

Millie glared. "I warned him, but he insisted."

"Obviously, lessons will be in order." He took Millie's hand. "How about we take a breather on the patio?"

"They put heaters out there," Hugh informed them. "Should be comfortable."

Stella and Hugh moved toward the dancers while Millie and Dane walked to the patio. "Do you need your coat?" Dane asked, wrapping his arm around her shoulder.

"No. I'm comfortable where I am."

"I have a Christmas present for you."

"You already told me. Yours is in the car."

"I think I want to give it to you now."

Warmth filled her heart. "It's midnight somewhere, isn't it?"

He pulled a long, slender box from the inside of his jacket and handed it to Millie.

She opened the unhinged side. A sparkling silver charm bracelet lay on a white satin cover.

"They're things that brought us together. The bakery and the bookstore." He nudged the book and cupcake. "The sign and a paintbrush. Here's a snowflake for your prank in the snow."

"A dog. That wasn't one of our pranks."

"She helped bring us closer."

Millie ran her finger across the charms. "They're delicate and detailed."

"I meet all manner of specialists in the book business. I had it made."

"In the past week? What about this one? Why the heart? I don't remember anything about that."

"Don't you remember stealing my heart? I'm head over heels about you." He slipped the bracelet from the box. She held her wrist in front of him. He looped the two ends around her and hooked the bracelet together. "I mean it, I'm falling in love with you."

"The final caper captures us both." Millie felt breathless.

"I think I'd like to hear you say the words."

"I'm falling in love with you, Baxter Dane."

He took her in his arms. "I don't like the name Baxter."

She grinned. "I'm sure I can say it in a way to change your mind."

He kissed her instead of arguing.

Magic of the night warred with the reality of baker hours. A slow dance, and Millie had to cover her mouth from a yawn. She felt Dane's husky laugh.

"Are you going to fall asleep in my arms?" They moved along with the music.

"I'm sorry. I was in the kitchen before five this morning getting things prepped."

He brushed his cheek against her forehead. "It's been an incredibly busy day."

"I don't think I'll make midnight."

"Do you have any free time tomorrow?"

"I might. What time are you getting together with your sister?"

"We aren't. She and Becca went to Pennsylvania to be with our parents. They'll all be down next week."

Millie stopped and stared at him. "So, what are you doing for Christmas?"

He shrugged. "Book and a chair."

She shook her head. "At Grandma Cooke's house. You'll join us."

"I don't want to intrude."

"You won't be. You have been invited, and because you have the fortune of being my date, you are guaranteed a seat at the table."

Dane tucked hair behind her ear before adjusting the Santa hat. "Millicent, I would be delighted to spend Christmas with you and your family."

"We, Baxter Dane, are blessed to have you."

They finished their dance.

32

Millie listened for the creek of the step as she moved to the front door of Aunt Bea's house. Luna wiggled in her arms.

Aunt Bea threw the door open. "Merry Christmas! I hate having to wait until you get here, now you girls no longer live at home." She started when she saw who stood beside Millie. "Well, hello, Mr. Dane."

"You can call me Dane, Aunt Bea," he replied, taking hold of the door. The ladies moved around him to go inside.

Aunt Bea beamed at Millie. "Are you…"

Millie sighed. "We are giving dating a try." She unhooked the dog then glanced at Dane. "See if we enjoy getting along more than annoying each other."

Aunt Bea engulfed her in a hug. "Oh, the annoying doesn't stop. Caring makes it more interesting"

Dane muttered, "tell me about it."

"Where's Stella?"

"Hugh picked her up." Millie handed the bag of goodies to Dane and pointed at the buffet table in the hallway. "You can set these there."

"We'll need another table," Aunt Bea teased.

"I don't have to stay," Dane said as he walked

away.

"Nonsense." Aunt Bea followed him. "There's always plenty of food. We'll find a spot for everyone to sit."

"I think it's getting colder outside," Stella declared as she and Hugh stepped through the front door. She rubbed her arms.

"Merry Christmas, do I hear my granddaughters?" Grandma Cooke sauntered into the crowded foyer, followed by Mr. Willard. Millie and Stella wrapped themselves around her, both laughing.

"Plenty of space in the living room," Mr. Willard declared in a loud, deep voice. "No need to be stuck here like sardines."

"Good plan," Millie agreed, hooking one arm around Grandma Cooke as they followed Mr. Willard. Luna raced between them, through to the living room.

Grandma Cooke turned. "Baxter Dane, is that you? Merry Christmas, young man. Are you here with my granddaughter?"

"Yes, ma'am," he placed a hand on Millie's shoulder.

"I will have to tell Dahlia when she arrives." The older woman beamed. "She owes me twenty dollars."

"For what?" Millie frowned.

"She thought it would take until after New Years for the two of you to get on the same path."

"You made a bet?" Stella laughed.

"You didn't," Millie protested at the same time.

But Grandma Cooke grinned, nodding. "After I told her about the gala."

Hugh moved through the room to Aunt Lettie. "They got you settled, I see."

"My friends and family take good care of me." The dog jumped up beside her. Hugh made to push Luna away, but Grandma Keyes shooed him. "I enjoy time with this fuzzy gal. Although, I am hungry. Is everyone here? Where is your sister?"

"Allison's in the kitchen," Millie pointed.

Aunt Bea looked at her watch. "Still waiting on Dahlia. It's unusual for her to be late. Hope everything's okay."

"Everything is lovely," Dahlia declared as she entered the living room. "Merry Christmas, indeed."

Millie did a double take at the tall gentleman standing beside Aunt Dahlia. "Mr. Allister?"

Dahlia wrapped her arm around his waist. "This is Lenny Allister," her accent skipped the r in his name. "I invited him to be my guest today. I know we always have plenty."

"Welcome," Millie smiled. "There's not a better home to visit for Christmas."

He gave a nervous smile. "From what I smell, you don't exaggerate."

"That's two more settings, Sylvia," Aunt Bea told her friend.

"We have a cart table next door," Mildred offered.

Aunt Bea motioned for Hugh and Dane. "There should be another leaf for the table in the hall closet. I think we can get everyone together."

They scavenged next door for chairs, but everyone managed a spot at the dining room table. Aunt Bea stood at the head. "Such a blessing to see love this Christmas. If my Al were here, he'd have a long story to tell before getting on with the prayer. Suffice to say this is a very merry Christmas with all of you in my home."

Dane raised a mug of wassail. "God bless us, everyone." He stole a kiss from Millie, which meant Hugh had to kiss Stella. Willard kissed Grandma Cooke's cheek, and Dahlia did the same to Allister. Laughter filled the room as trays of food were passed. Luna waited at the edge of the table for her share of the yummy smells.

Other books by Laurie Boulden:

Hidden Gems
Jewel of Jericho

Laurie Boulden is Assistant Professor of Elementary Education at Warner University. She volunteers time with youth and ladies' ministries at Trinity Baptist Church. She is a member of Word Weavers International and has attended the Florida Christian Writers Conference five years. She has won awards multiple years in the novel category for Biblical fiction, fantasy and science fiction, and contemporary romance. She won Writer of the Year in 2016. She recently completed a Master of Art in Creative Writing and English. Her interests lie in writing as well as teaching others to write. A good story deserves a good telling.

Made in United States
Orlando, FL
27 November 2021

10800829R00168